By Eva Muñoz

MODA NOSTRA
Bang On Trend

Published by Harmony Ink Press

Impulse

INSHARI CHRONICLES
I Dare You to Break Curfew

Published by DREAMSPINNER PRESS
www.dreamspinnerpress.com

EVA MUÑOZ

BANG ON TREND

Published by

DREAMSPINNER PRESS

5032 Capital Circle SW, Suite 2, PMB# 279, Tallahassee, FL 32305-7886 USA
www.dreamspinnerpress.com

Bang On Trend
© 2021 Eva Muñoz

Cover Art
© 2021 L.C. Chase
http://www.lcchase.com
Cover content is for illustrative purposes only and any person depicted on the cover is a model.

Trade Paperback ISBN: 978-1-64405-930-2
Digital ISBN: 978-1-64405-929-6
Trade Paperback published June 2021
First Edition
v. 1.0

Printed in the United States of America
∞
This paper meets the requirements of
ANSI/NISO Z39.48-1992 (Permanence of Paper).

CHAPTER ONE
BRIONI

MILO MCLAREN hated Valentine's Day. The morbid commercialization of love made him sick. It was the time when flowers, chocolates, and cheesy greeting cards became depression triggers for the currently unattached. Ah, good ol' Singles Awareness Day. The only reason he wasn't wallowing in a self-imposed pity party was because—

Ding.

The elevator doors opened to the offices of *Rebel*, the popular fashion magazine. Besides the typical work frenzy he walked into on a daily basis, the reception area and glass-walled bullpen where the cubicles were located were bedecked in every conceivable Valentine's Day paraphernalia. Love vomited all over the place, and no surface was spared.

Cupids shooting magic arrows hung from the ceiling. Hearts clung to the walls. And red roses were *everywhere*. Each employee desk boasted a vase of them, standing out on the cluttered surface. The cloying scent stung his nostrils. Even the clothing racks had red bows tied to each end.

The urge to run in the opposite direction consumed him, but to miss work because of his personal issues was unforgivable. So instead, he prayed, but his prayer for a swift death was interrupted by a wave of confetti and the shouted words of "Happy Valentine's—"

The greeting cut off at about the same time the toxic scowl he reserved for magazine layout day and uppity diva models manifested, contorting his classically handsome features into a demon mask only a handful of people were immune to. The two standing before him

1

weren't included in that group. They immediately paled and took several steps back as he exited the elevator.

"Who died?" Kasey, the top-knotted, hipster-glasses-wearing receptionist asked, referring to Milo's black-on-black vintage-inspired Marc Jacobs suit.

"My dignity," he said, sliding his scowl toward the art director's assistant.

The always colorful Garret, in suspenders and plaid, whose hair currently screamed pink, cringed before he leaped forward and began dusting gold and red shiny squares off Milo's shoulders.

"I'm so sorry," he muttered on repeat. "Please don't fire me."

Milo's confetti shower chilled him to the bone. He took a deep breath and enunciated each word he spoke. "Please tell me you haven't been throwing confetti at each person who comes out of this elevator?"

He narrowed his gaze at the culprits who thought they were being cute. The idea that their boss might have walked out to this in her couture was enough to make him draw blood.

Kasey shook her head so hard he was afraid her topknot would fly off. "Only you. Promise!" She waved her hands for emphasis… or as a defensive maneuver against possible attacks.

He swatted away Garret's fretting hands. "And why did you two think I needed glitter rain this morning?"

Clasping his hands together, Garret said, "You've been absolutely gloomy. Valentine's Day should be a happy occasion. Why don't you let me take you out tonight?"

"Hey!" Kasey scowled. "That was my idea. Go out with me instead!" she demanded of Milo.

A long and protracted sigh left Milo's lungs once the realization hit that his two friends were just looking out for him, for his happiness. On a regular day, he would have found their antics cute. But not today of all days. Not today. He willed the annoyance away as he ran his fingers through his thick chestnut waves and dislodged several more foil squares.

"As much as I enjoy playing for both teams, I'm not one to shit where I eat, and I'd advise the both of you to do the same." He gestured at the floor with a sweep of his hand. "Clean this up before Cassandra gets here."

"She's already here," Kasey said as Garret scampered away to, Milo assumed, fetch a broom.

"What?" His heart made a beeline for his throat while he checked his watch. "She doesn't usually get in at this hour."

"She's been here since six."

And it was already eight. A different kind of annoyance ignited in his chest. He always got here before the boss. *Always.*

"Did she tell you why?" he asked, not bothering to mask the rising panic in his tone.

Rebel had no set working hours. Schedules varied depending on the task assigned. From editors down to assistants, staff came in when they needed and left when they were done. Days could start as early as six, sometimes earlier, and could end as late as midnight.

There were special circumstances, such as a double-issue layout, where no one went home at all for two or three days straight. The longest anyone had ever stayed at the office was a week, and that was because someone accidentally downloaded a virus into their network. It ate up everything needed for the coming issue.

Milo had blocked out most of that incident, yet he still experienced facial tics when he remembered it. Safe to say that idiot no longer worked for *Rebel*—or anywhere in the fashion industry, for that matter.

"She's been on a conference call all...."

The second the words *conference* and *call* were uttered, Milo didn't bother listening to the rest. He hurried to his desk outside Cassandra's frosted-glass office. The door was closed. The dark silhouette inside indicated her presence. *Shit.*

He didn't bother to remove his coat and scarf as he dumped his bag on the floor, bent over his computer, and cued up today's schedule. He cursed under his breath and inhaled sharply, his lips disappearing into a tight line. At the top of the list was the conference call. He'd been so distracted this past week that he'd completely forgotten about the prep.

Paris Fashion Week in March was one of Cassandra's biggest events of the year. It took at least six months to plan and coordinate the trip. Logistics alone were a nightmare. Meetings, fashion shows, dinners with designers… the list of things to do went on and on. As her executive assistant, Milo held sole responsibility for pulling everything off without so much as a hiccup.

Instant disappointment punched through his chest. *Totally dropped the ball on this one.* He bowed his head and massaged the back of his neck as he gathered his courage to enter the lion's den. His hatred for this day had gotten him into this mess, and like Kasey and Garret cleaning up the confetti, he'd have to sweep his way out.

He clicked Print and straightened as the schedule spat out. He pulled off his scarf and shrugged out of his coat as he composed the appropriate apology for being late. Much groveling might be involved. Maybe even some self-flagellation.

Milo swallowed and tugged on the lapels of his suit jacket before he grabbed the schedule from the printer tray and rounded his desk to stand in front of what the interns called "the door to hell." Many an onion-skinned person had run out of this office in tears. Even Milo had shed a drop or two when Cassandra was feeling particularly vicious.

Not bothering with a deep breath, he knocked once and pushed in. The best editor in chief in the business stood behind her desk with arms crossed. She wore a sleek suit with exaggerated shoulders and covered entirely in peacock feathers. One of the perks of her position was having all her clothes custom made by the best designers.

She was a goddess, and the designers were suppliants making offerings so she would shower them with her blessings. Making it into the pages of *Rebel* meant making it in the fashion world. So yeah, keeping Cassandra happy was a full-time job for *everyone.*

She spoke in rapid-fire French just as he nudged the door closed. Someone at the other end replied via the phone's speaker, and she shook her head. Her silver hair, cut in a severe bob with razor-sharp bangs across her forehead, followed the movement. She spoke again and crooked a finger at Milo.

The walls of his throat closed at the sharp look she gave him. She was a strikingly beautiful woman. If she didn't love "behind the scenes," she could easily have been a model like his mother.

He approached her desk, which was cluttered with fashion magazines, newspapers, and sample swatches. While she continued to argue with whoever it was, he clipped her schedule onto a board hanging on the wall and then proceeded to tidy up. Over the years he had trained himself to anticipate Cassandra's every need.

Magazines with Post-its were always left open. Magazines without them were closed and stacked on the left side of the desk. Newspapers were folded and went on the right side.

He picked up the cloth swatches, and Cassandra pointed at the rack of clothing samples slated for the fall issue. He nodded and busied himself with matching pieces of fabric. Looking at the selection, it seemed military-inspired leather jackets were making a comeback, but instead of the usual camo, they came in jewel tones. That meant silver jewelry and chunky belts.

Milo prided himself on knowing how to predict trends. It took him years to get the nuances, but when he did, it was like opening a door into a magical world not many were able to enter. With his father always away on business, his supermodel mother had no choice but to bring him along on photo shoots and fashion shows. He grew up among models, photographers, makeup artists, and designers. Instead of trucks and blocks, he played with makeup brushes and helped pull together outfits.

Being in the fashion industry seemed like the perfect fit for him from the get-go. An internship at eighteen had propelled him to his present esteemed position. A million people would kill to be in his Prada loafers. It didn't matter that his boss also happened to be his mother's best friend and his *de facto* godmother, or that his father owned the publishing company the magazine belonged to.

Nepotism might have been in play when he was starting out, but he didn't get to where he was now without clawing his way up.

Outsiders thought the fashion industry was all clothes and pretty things when in fact it was far more bloodthirsty than a night inside the octagon of a UFC fight. In his world the gloves were off, there were no rules, and may the best trend win.

Once the swatches were put away, he picked up Cassandra's slim coffee cup and brought it to her personal Nespresso machine. He placed the empty cup below the nozzle, popped in an espresso capsule, and pressed the Start button. As it gurgled and dripped, the scent of coffee filled the office.

Milo felt more at home here than in his own apartment. The walls were covered with all the latest sketches from designers, all the furniture was sleek and modern, reflecting the tastes of their owner, and the view of the city was simply breathtaking.

He was staring absentmindedly into the distance at the swath of green that made up Central Park when slim arms wrapped around his waist from behind. Cassandra rested her chin on his shoulder, and he braced himself for cutting words. Instead, he got a kiss on the cheek before she let go and stepped back. He turned around, a frown forming on his lips and forehead.

"Oh, my dear boy," she said, pursing her lips and cupping his face with both hands.

Instant warmth chased away his fear. "I'm sorry for being late."

The slap was swift and unexpected. It was hard enough to sting but not hard enough to leave a mark. She wagged a finger at him. There was the scary woman he'd grown up with.

"I understand the special circumstances surrounding this day, which is why I will forgive you for your tardiness," she said in a clipped tone.

He nodded and closed a hand over the one she still kept on his cheek. "Won't happen again. The conference call—"

"That is no longer your concern," she interrupted him. "Kenji Suzuki is already at the studio for his shoot. As I have more calls to make before I can join him, I would like you to—"

"I understand," he interrupted her in return, stepping out of reach.

6

"Very good."

He smirked. "I'll keep him happy until you get there."

Her lips quirked in what passed for a smile as she waved him away.

Relief settled on Milo's shoulders once he left the office. He knew why Cassandra sent him to entertain the up-and-coming Japanese designer instead of one of her editors. He'd spent a year in Japan.

At the same time, this was a test. If he couldn't pull this off, then he wasn't worthy of climbing the ranks to become the next editor in chief. God only knew what Cassandra would put him through then—most likely demote him to taking care of the interns. A shudder went through him. He'd take a slap any day, thank you very much.

He grabbed his tablet from his desk and hurried back toward the elevator. Not a speck of confetti anywhere. Kasey was already taking calls behind the semicircle of the reception desk.

Good. A semblance of normalcy had returned to his workplace. All he had to do now was ignore the decorations for the rest of the day.

"Going to the studios?" Garret asked, sidling closer, a manila envelope and his own tablet in his hands.

"I have Suzuki-babysitting duty until Cassandra finishes her calls." He glanced up at the numbers counting down on the LCD panel above them.

"Have you seen the House of Suzuki dresses?" Garret gushed. "I still can't believe they're made of hemp."

The September issue of *Rebel* was all about innovation in fashion. Hemp was the hot fabric of the moment, and no one manipulated the coarse material better than Kenji Suzuki. His designs took on shapes and forms any origami master would be proud of.

The art of paper folding was most evident in the centerpiece of his collection, which boasted a thousand cranes and was connected to the tradition that whoever folded a thousand paper cranes would have a wish granted. It was also connected to eternal good luck. Milo had only seen pictures of the designs. To actually get to see the dresses in person had him as giddy as a kid on Christmas Day.

"Each dress is a total work of art," Garret mused as they entered the elevator. "And worth a small fortune. I heard actresses are already lining up to wear his clothes for awards season."

"Why are you headed to the studios?" Milo asked as he pushed the button for the floor they were headed to.

There must have been some heat in his tone, because Garret flinched. "Cassandra chew you out for being late?"

He shook his head. "I'm sorry for the way I acted earlier."

"Just because today is—"

"Let's not rehash." He sighed. "So, why are you headed to the studios? Please don't tell me it's to ogle the Suzuki designs."

"That," Garret said with a wide smile, "*and* I have to deliver these proof changes to the photographer of the autumn jackets spread."

"Your boss changed his mind again?" Milo asked in reference to the picky and often prickly art director.

Garret rolled his eyes.

"Cassandra's not going to like that. We're already over budget for that shoot." A genuine grin spread across his lips. "Looking forward to the bloodbath at the next editorial meeting."

"I'll bring the popcorn."

He and Garret stepped out of the elevator into a long corridor filled with framed, blown-up covers of *Rebel*. The best of the best hung along these walls, including his mother, who had graced the cover no less than ten times throughout her modeling career. Milo stopped at the one Stella von Stein was best known for—a close-up of her gorgeous face.

She had no makeup on except for pink lips and a shaved head. Her wide-set hazel eyes—so much like his—stared at him unflinchingly. Besides the chestnut color of his hair that he inherited from his father, everything else came from his mother—perfectly symmetrical features and the kind of full lips people paid plastic surgeons good money for. He came from a rare gene pool. Cassandra always joked that if he wore a dress, he could pass as his mother's sister.

"The Breast Cancer Awareness issue," Garret murmured in reverence.

8

Milo remembered the day the doctors gave his mother the diagnosis. Instead of panicking about the potential end of her career, she posed nude post-surgery and chemo, baring it all for the world to see. Bravest thing he'd ever seen anyone do. He was so proud of her that his chest ached.

Unwilling to confront the swell of emotion, Milo resumed his trek toward the main studio at the end of the hall. He checked the shoot's location on his tablet and then pushed through the double doors. Garret followed him.

They stepped into the whirl of activity without missing a beat, used to the hustle of a photo shoot. The makeup station lined one side of the thousand-square-foot space where artists painted frantically on human canvases and racks of exquisite clothing lined the other. In a corner sat equipment and photography gear.

At the far end were the craft services tables with large silver platters. No one dared touch food and then touch clothing. A girl was once fired for picking up a cube of cheese before she handed a silk skirt to a model. The designer wasn't happy.

Speaking of a designer, Milo pulled up Kenji's profile on the screen and quickly searched for him in the melee. Garret pointed him out. He looked pale in a crisp white suit and had lavender hair combed to one side to bare the shaved side. He wore burgundy lipstick and false eyelashes. His arms were crossed, and he bit down on the long fingernail of his pinky while he watched the model pose in front of the camera in a soft pink structural dress that resembled a giant water lily.

"Who's that?" Garret asked.

Judging from his friend's hum of appreciation, he was referring to the tall man in a gray three-piece Brioni suit Milo had last seen in the spring collection catalog. That suit wouldn't be available in stores until next year. The fact that he wore it meant he had considerable pull and a lot of money.

He stood beside Kenji with the poise of someone who knew what wearing a good suit could do. He had his hands in his pockets, which emphasized how broad his shoulders were. A linebacker couldn't have done any better. Milo had worked with more than enough male models to know that the way the perfectly tailored suit sat contentedly on his body meant he sported some serious muscle underneath.

"I don't know," he finally said.

For some reason he was unable to tear his gaze away from Kenji's companion. His jet-black hair was combed away from a face that boasted high cheekbones and a clean-shaven square jaw. It wasn't his stunning looks alone; it was the air that surrounded him.

He was a man who stood on solid ground and was comfortable in his own skin—someone who didn't care what others thought. At least that was Milo's impression of him at first glance. Confidence personified.

"Well, he's hot," Garret added matter-of-factly.

"Don't you have work to do?" Milo reminded him, scowling.

"I will leave if you promise to tell me his name later. Extra points if you get his number."

Ignoring his too-eager friend, Milo stepped forward and dusted off his Japanese. He hoped to hell he wouldn't mess up.

Kenji noticed him first and eyed Milo. Then he grinned as he whispered to his companion, "Kare wa utsukushīde wa arimasen?"

A sudden blush washed over his face. He'd just been called beautiful by a designer with features so feminine they rivaled those of the models in this shoot. He stood frozen, not because of the cool assessment that came from the man in the Brioni suit, but from staring into steel blue irises that seemed to undress him and see through him all at once.

CHAPTER TWO
BLUE

UNABLE TO move, yet drawn forward by some invisible force, Milo didn't know what to do. He didn't usually lose confidence in himself, having dealt with models, celebrities, and designers alike without batting an eyelash. Yet in this instance, no matter how much his brain screamed at him to say something, his gaze remained locked on the stranger's haunting eyes. The Japanese called them *mugen no ao* or infinite blue, like the skies over Hokkaido or Okinawa.

Then he said something in a deep and sexy voice that pulled Milo out of his stupor. "Kenji-kun sonna hanashi o yamete. Kare wa hazukashiku narimashita."

Kenji threw his head back and laughed. "Sono yō na koto shitenai yo."

They acted as if Milo couldn't understand them, talking about embarrassing him and Kenji denying that he had. This pissed him off enough to regain his composure.

In equally measured Japanese, he greeted them both a good morning and bowed from the waist, as was customary when meeting a business associate. Then he launched into introducing himself and explaining that Cassandra was currently finishing up some calls and that she sent him to assist them in whatever they may need until she arrived.

"*Ara*," Kenji exclaimed, touching his cheek. Then, still speaking Japanese, he said, "I apologize. I didn't know you spoke Nihongo. You're quite good."

Milo straightened to catch a glimpse of how impressed the designer was before the emotion was replaced by the earlier assessing mask he wore. His friend continued to stare, stone-faced, but Milo thought it best to ignore him or he might be struck speechless again.

He plastered on a cordial smile when he said, "I spent a year in Tokyo and picked up a few things."

Kenji's eyes sparkled with mischief. "I like a boy who understands my desires."

This brought another blush to Milo's cheeks, because when said in Japanese, "Watashi no yokubō o rikai shitekureru otokonoko ga suki," it sounded so sensual, as though Kenji meant more to his words than just expressing his gratefulness at having someone anticipate his needs.

"I'm at your service," Milo said around a suddenly dry mouth.

"Oh, I'm so sorry. Look at me forgetting my manners." Kenji gestured toward his tall, incredibly handsome companion. It would be rude if Milo didn't look at him, so he schooled his features into a professional mask and returned his gaze to the man who had never stopped staring at him. "Let me introduce Kazuhiko Yukifumi. He's my best friend and business partner."

Milo's eyes widened. An eight-syllable Japanese name? He must come from a hard-core traditional family to walk around with a name like that.

Remembering his own manners, he bowed again and said, "It's nice to meet you, Yukifumi-san." Adding the honorific at the end was also customary when meeting a new acquaintance. It was akin to adding "Mr." or "Ms." when addressing someone.

Speaking again in a voice that commanded instant attention, Kenji's companion said in English, "Enough. We're not in Japan. Let's dispense with the formalities. Kenji was just having some fun...." He glanced at his friend and then returned those piercing eyes to Milo. "It seems it was at your expense. I apologize. Please, you can call me Kaz."

For a moment Milo could do nothing but stare... *again*. There was something so mesmerizing about him. The way he spoke, so calm and precise, took Milo's breath away. His tone belied his Japanese roots, yet there wasn't a hint of an accent, which told Milo he'd spent

12

time in the States as well. In fact, his words were so neutral that Milo couldn't place where he was from.

"Oh, Yuki-kun, you're no fun."

Thank God for Kenji and his ability to return Milo to the present. He caught the nickname Kenji used for Kaz. It wasn't uncommon to take part of someone's last name in reference to them, especially in instances when said last name had multiple syllables. But it also told Milo that they might not be close enough for Kenji to refer to Kaz by his first name.

A certain intimacy between individuals must be reached before that could happen. Kaz calling Kenji by his first name showed his more Western inclinations.

"Be that as it may," he finally replied, switching to English as well, "I'd like to keep my job, and keeping my job means I call you Mr. Yukifumi."

Kaz narrowed his cool gaze at him and nodded once, possibly in acceptance of the continued formality between them. Milo wouldn't have it any other way.

"It's nice to meet you, Milo McLaren," Kaz said.

His name coming from Kaz's lips sounded like leaves rustling in the wind. It sent a shiver down Milo's spine.

HOURS LATER, Milo sat at a table for two in his favorite restaurant, surrounded by couples celebrating the longest damn day in the history of long days. He used a reservation he'd made six months in advance for the sole purpose of stuffing himself with the tastiest baby back ribs in order to numb the gnawing pain at the center of his chest. He considered it a fitting reward for surviving half a dozen Candygrams and the multitude of flowers and chocolates delivered to the *Rebel* offices all day.

Even he received a bouquet of yellow roses and a box of Godiva… from his mother. If Kasey hadn't taken the box and the blooms away, he would have slashed his wrists with a letter opener. Unfortunately for him, the decorations followed him here too. Red, pink, and silver streamers dangled from the ceiling. How it wasn't considered a fire hazard baffled him.

He wiped his hands with a Wet-Nap provided by a waiter as a massive platter was set in the middle of his table. His mouth watered at the sight—a whole slab, slathered in the richest honey barbecue sauce. To undercut the sweet-savory combination, he had asked for a side order of blue cheese dressing. No side dishes, no carbs, no veggies. Just the ribs. Straight up.

"Will that be all, sir?" the tuxedo-clad waiter asked, unable to suppress the skeptical look on his pinched face.

"Yes." Milo handed the man his plate and pulled the entire platter toward him. Not bothering with utensils, he separated the first rib from the rack with his fingers and dove right in, though he almost choked because of the horrified glances from couples nearest his table.

"If there is anything else—"

He cut off the waiter's words with a wave of the second rib he had liberated. But just before the man could walk away, he said, "I might need another order of this. I'll let you know."

"Very good, sir. Enjoy."

"Oh, I will," he muttered. Then he took a bite of his third rib, which he dipped into the ramekin of blue cheese.

By the time Milo was halfway through the platter, a figure stood by the vacant chair opposite him. "That looks good."

Rib between his teeth, he whipped his head up to catch a glimpse of Kaz, still looking polished and gorgeous in his Brioni suit. Surely Milo had barbecue sauce all over his mouth and chin. *Oh God.* He might as well dig a grave and lie in it.

In embarrassment at having been caught pigging out, he covered his mouth and said, "Mr. Yukifumi, what are you doing here?"

A raven-wing eyebrow twitched up. "May I join you? It seems I picked the wrong night to dine out."

Swallowing hard, Milo sat in complete disbelief. If he said yes, then how could he continue eating with abandon? But if he said no and it got back to Cassandra that he refused Kenji Suzuki's business partner… he didn't want to imagine the consequences.

Picking the lesser of two evils, he nodded and gestured with barbeque-sauce-covered fingers toward the chair opposite him. Unthinking, he popped his thumb into his mouth and sucked. Kaz paused in the act of pulling out the chair to stare at him.

The heat in that look unnerved Milo until he realized what he'd been doing. He pulled out his thumb with an audible pop and quickly picked up another Wet-Nap. Slippery fingers made opening the plastic packet a chore, and it didn't help that his hands shook. The self-consciousness he'd been feeling around Kaz all day had returned.

When the packet slipped out of his fingers a third time, a large hand picked it up. Before Milo could protest, Kaz had already ripped open the plastic and was handing him the moist napkin. He reached for it with a slight bow and murmured his gratitude. Then he proceeded to concentrate on cleaning his fingers and mouth. So much for stuffing his face with ribs.

Kaz gestured for a waiter and ordered a bottle of wine. After the waiter left, he asked, "Why did you stop?" He indicated the half-eaten slab. "Am I interrupting something? Perhaps you're waiting for your date tonight?"

Like Kasey that morning, Milo shook his head so hard it was a miracle he didn't give himself whiplash.

"What about you? No chocolates delivered to you today?" he asked back, referring to the Japanese tradition of women giving men chocolates on Valentine's Day as a sign of affection.

The men had White Day, which was March 14, to reciprocate by giving gifts like cookies, jewelry, white chocolate, white lingerie, or marshmallows.

A smirk changed the stoic expression Kaz wore into one of roguish appeal. Ah, the man was as mouthwatering as the ribs. The image of licking him from head to toe made Milo sit up straighter, but before Kaz could respond to his question, the waiter returned with a bottle Milo recognized.

It was one of the most expensive wines on the list. Since it was ordered at his table, did that mean he had to pay for it? This wasn't exactly a work dinner, so using his expense account was out of the question.

"Care to join me?" Kaz asked, indicating the second empty glass the waiter held.

"I don't really drink wine," he said, shifting in his seat. If he remembered correctly, that was a fifteen-hundred-dollar bottle.

His sudden dinner guest must have picked up on his unease because he asked the waiter to leave. Once they were alone, he took a sip from his glass and said, "You have to let me pay for dinner. It's the least I can do for sharing your table with me."

"What?" Milo jolted. "I can't let you do that." Maybe he could write it off as a business expense?

"Please, I insist." He placed the wineglass on the table and swirled its contents. "I interrupted your dinner by joining you."

"But...." Milo swallowed the rest of his refusal.

What was one dinner, right? He nodded again, and his shoulders drooped slightly in defeat. On a regular day, he would have a better handle on himself. It was just today that he wasn't feeling quite his usual self.

"You don't have to stop on my account," Kaz said. "Those ribs look really good."

Milo's stomach did an unexpected flip. Kaz possessed the kind of confidence of someone who could afford to buy Brioni suits and expensive wine. He'd grown up around it with his father and his business associates.

Men with money. Men with power. They all seemed to walk and talk the same—self-assured, solid, slightly arrogant. A part of him liked it, which put him at ease enough to go back to eating.

"So, you're Japanese," he said after swallowing a new bite. He saw it now as he looked at Kaz up close—the slight slant of his eyes, the straightness of the black hair falling across his forehead, angular features.

16

"Born in Tokyo." Kaz leaned back in his seat, and his hand never left the stem of the wineglass while the other rested on his thigh. "Went to grade school here, high school there, college here."

"That's a lot of back and forth. No wonder you don't have an accent when speaking either Nihongo or English. Your tone's very neutral." He locked gazes with him. "I don't want to state the obvious…."

"You mean these." He pointed at his blue eyes. "My mother was from Kansas."

"Was?" The question slipped out without him having to think twice.

At the hardening of Kaz's gaze, Milo searched for a change of topic. He was used to gauging the emotions of the people he dealt with and doing what was necessary to avoid potentially awkward or sticky situations. Models, especially, were particularly temperamental.

Ruffling Kaz's feathers wasn't on the agenda. If he didn't want to talk about anything personal, they would switch to business.

"How did you get into fashion?"

The tension in the air quickly eased. Milo silently commended himself for getting it right as Kaz said, "I'm actually not. Kenji is the one in the fashion business."

"But you're his business partner."

The more they spoke, the more at ease Milo became. Kaz didn't seem as intimidating as he had that morning, maybe because of the calm cadence of his speech. It was almost monotone yet strangely soothing.

"Silent partner," he corrected.

"So, what do you do?"

He raised his wineglass and took another sip. "Imports and exports."

Milo's next question was interrupted by the arrival of a leggy blond in a flowing silk dress the color of the wine Kaz enjoyed. The skirt moved with the sway of her hips. He didn't have time to hope that she hadn't seen him, because she was already making her way to their table with purposeful strides.

"Milo?" she asked with a stunning smile.

"Celeste." Her name tasted foul in his mouth as he pushed back from the table and stood up.

He reached out a hand, but she shimmied closer and gave each of his cheeks quick air kisses. His heart dropped to the pit of his stomach the second her signature floral scent entered his nose. God, he missed her.

The thought hit him like a sledgehammer. Even a year later, her effect on him remained the same.

"It's so good to see you!" Her bubbly demeanor hadn't changed either.

Searching for something to say other than "You look good," his gaze found Kaz, who silently watched the exchange. "Celeste, this is Mr. Kazuhiko Yukifumi. He's Kenji Suzuki's business partner."

"You're Japanese?" she asked with genuine curiosity.

That was one of the things he'd loved about her—the openness, the innocence in everything she did. Then she greeted Kaz in Nihongo.

Kaz stood up and took her hand. He brought her knuckles to his lips, bringing a blush to Celeste's cheeks. He murmured something about speaking the language beautifully, and she giggled. Before Milo could feel jealousy at having another man touch her, he noticed the large diamond on her finger. Immediate hurt smacked him upside the head.

"You're getting married?" He could barely get the words out.

Celeste treated him to a wide grin as she bounced in place, showing him the ring. "Isn't it crazy? You should meet him."

A wave of nausea hit Milo, and he staggered.

"I think the wine has gone to your head," Kaz said, immediately moving to his side and lending him support by closing a steady hand around his arm.

"Oh." Celeste's lips actually formed an O, concern marring her pretty features. "That's odd since Milo holds his liquor better than anyone."

"I should really take him home."

Good thing Kaz held him up, because Milo could no longer feel his legs. In fact, he could no longer feel much of anything.

"It was good seeing you again, Milo," she said to him.

He could only nod as Kaz led him away from their table.

"But the bill," he was finally able to say when they reached the restaurant entrance where a long line of people waited to be seated.

"Don't worry about it. Can you stand without falling over?"

The ground refused to feel solid beneath him. "She's getting married."

Kaz tightened his hold on Milo's arm. "I think you need a drink."

"Make that two."

CHAPTER THREE
BAR

KAZ'S DRIVER eased the town car to the curb outside the bar Milo had suggested. The entire drive had given him a chance to bury the roiling nausea caused by flashbacks of his life, but he was still left with boiling anger. Celeste was getting fucking married a year after…. He couldn't even bring himself to think of it without exploding or going on an insane rampage through the city.

Love sucked.

Having a day to celebrate it sucked worse. Finding out the girl he once loved was getting married on said day was cause for damage. Serious damage. Preferably to a bottle of tequila.

The second the car glided to a stop, he threw open the door and headed straight into Santino—an upscale hole-in-the-wall that harkened back to the quiet bar days. No dance floor here.

The bouncer outside nodded as Milo approached and knocked once on the door. It was members only, for people who liked to drink alone and not be bothered.

"He's with me," he said, hiking a thumb over his shoulder at Kaz, who he assumed trailed behind him.

The bouncer nodded again just as the door slid open. Milo headed straight for the massive mahogany bar that dominated the space. The lack of Valentine's Day décor made him feel marginally better. Thank God for tiny miracles.

Unfortunately, the lack of people drinking themselves to an early grave showed just how in love the entire city was. The nausea he'd kicked came back with a new level of pathetic. Was he the only brokenhearted SOB in a city of millions? Impossible, but it sure seemed that way.

Peter, the bartender, grinned at him, but the second he recognized the blood in Milo's expression, he immediately filled a shot glass with the most expensive tequila they had in stock. Milo threw back its contents. The golden liquid carved a burning trail down his throat, easing his rising temper. He slammed the shot glass down, and Peter immediately filled it again. The guy was getting a ridiculously large tip tonight.

"Straight up?" he asked, pointing at the salt shaker and the wooden bowl full of lime slices.

In response, Milo downed the second shot without a glance at the tequila training wheels.

"Straight up, then." He filled the glass again. "Would you like to drink it straight out of the bottle to save time?"

"I don't appreciate your sarcasm today," Milo growled, rethinking the huge tip. He took a seat on the leather barstool as he swallowed the third shot.

Finally the hot anger turned into warm annoyance. The tequila was doing its job. A few more and he would be in happy oblivion. He couldn't wait. With the ribs in his stomach, it would take most of the bottle before he was good and drunk. And hopefully stupid.

What started off as a night of eating his feelings away had turned into getting plastered until he blacked out and all the events prior to arriving at Santino ceased to exist.

Peter whistled. "Who screwed you over?"

Milo glared. "You don't need to keep pouring. Just leave the bottle, and I'll take care of myself."

The bartender shrugged and moved a step toward Milo's left, where Kaz had taken his own seat. "I'm assuming you're a guest of this fool?"

Kaz said in that deep, serious voice of his, "I'll have a scotch, neat."

"What kind?" Peter asked back.

"Top shelf black label," Milo answered for him after he downed his fourth shot. He glanced sideways at Kaz, who nodded and treated him to the same assessing gaze he'd given when they first met that morning. "This one is on me. And don't argue. Your money won't be accepted here, because you're not a member."

Kaz looked at Peter, who confirmed Milo's statement with a nod as he slid the glass of scotch toward him. Milo slipped off the barstool and indicated one of the more private booths with a tilt of his head.

Wrapping a large hand around his drink, Kaz unfolded his impressive height off the stool and sauntered over to the booth with the swagger of a man who owned any room he was in, even an empty one. Milo took a moment to study his broad shoulders and the torso that tapered to slim hips and a nice ass. Then he closed his fingers around the neck of the tequila bottle and followed. He slid into the opposite bench of their booth.

"It might not be my place to tell you this, but shouldn't you at least think of slowing down?" Like a man who had all night to spend with someone about to get slobbering drunk, Kaz took a languid sip of his drink.

Milo covered an unattractive burp with the crook of his elbow, then said, "The drunker I get, the better I will feel."

His impromptu drinking companion snorted. "Said every alcoholic in the world."

To make his point, he swallowed another shot. He'd lost count by then. That was good. Losing count meant he was well on his way to being blackout drunk.

"This is for one night only. Trust me."

The soft lighting and brick interior gave the bar a masculine feel that fit Kaz well. Through hooded eyes, Milo stared at him from across the table.

"So...." Kaz tilted his glass toward him. "What are we drinking to?"

He refilled his shot glass and raised it. "To bitches who break your heart."

They touched glasses.

Kaz took another sip from his scotch and fished out a red-and-white pack of cigarettes and a Zippo with a dragon design from his inside jacket pocket. Only at Santino was smoking indoors still tolerated. The owner must be paying someone off to avoid fines. Milo didn't bother stopping Kaz when, with practiced moves, he tapped out a cigarette and sandwiched it between his lips. Then he flipped the lighter open and sharply turned the wheel with his thumb.

The flame danced for a moment. Seconds later, he exhaled, filling their space with smoke. The entire process was hypnotic. Milo admired the man's balls for not caring if he minded. In truth, he didn't. Models smoked like chimneys.

"What's the story?" Kaz asked after another drag. "It's obvious Celeste is more than just a friend."

Milo was sufficiently drunk for the walls to come down. Soon the loss of his inhibitions would follow. But before things got crazy, talking it through in drunken commiseration seemed like just what he needed.

"Celeste and I started going out my junior year of college. She was the best damn thing that ever happened in my life. Before her, I was just coasting along, content to keep moving forward without a real goal in mind. She was the one who convinced me to aim to become the editor in chief of *Rebel* after Cassandra retires." He shook his head in disappointment. "She showed me what I could do if I applied myself."

With an unreadable expression, Kaz listened. He nodded once in a while to show Milo he was paying attention, as though the seriousness of his features weren't an indicator of his rapt interest. So Milo continued between more shots.

"I was so in love with her that I was willing to move to Tokyo for a year when she got a paid internship there, just so we wouldn't have to do the long-distance thing."

"Ah, that explains your proficiency in Nihongo."

"Damn straight. Hers too." He slapped the tabletop and welcomed the sting in his palm. "Three years into our relationship, I was ready to settle down and start making babies with her. Or so I thought. You saw her tonight. Wasn't she the most beautiful thing on two legs you've ever seen?"

"I've seen better," Kaz muttered into his second glass of scotch, which Peter had sent over, along with an ashtray.

"Well, to me, she was the sunshine after a long winter. I was fucking crazy about her." He snorted. "I had everything planned. Valentine's Day. Reserved the best table at our favorite restaurant. I even had the ring. Harry Winston. A karat for each year we were together. Princess cut—"

"Because she was your princess," Kaz interrupted, disgust clear in his statement.

"You're getting it." Milo had guzzled enough of the tequila that his long-awaited numbness had finally arrived. He could get through the next part without breaking to pieces. "Everything was going smoothly. I was in my best Armani, and she was in this sexy emerald green Stella McCartney I borrowed from the *Rebel* closet. I pre-ordered all her favorite food, including the baked Alaska she loved that I completely abhorred."

"Don't tell me, the ring was in the dessert."

"Hell no!" He licked at the tequila that didn't quite make it all the way into his mouth. "I wasn't going to leave a ring like that in the hands of the waitstaff. I had it tucked inside my breast pocket, waiting for the right moment. Little did I know she had plans of her own."

He shook his head ruefully and sighed long and loud. "She waited until the middle of dessert. With a serious expression, she reached across the table for my hand. When I moved to lace our fingers together and she refused, it should have been my first red flag."

The tequila inched from comforting to sickening as the line of his lips tightened. The room started to spin like that tornado ride he forgot the name of at the state fair—slow at first until it reached full barf-inducing momentum. "With a serious face, she began telling me that in the last six months she'd met someone else and had been seeing him behind my back. I was so shocked all I could do was stare."

Kaz cursed under his breath in Japanese and scratched his eyebrow with a thumb. The smoke from his second cigarette curled toward the ceiling.

"*Kuso* is right," he repeated. "Afterward, she got up and walked out. When I got home, all her stuff was gone. She'd packed and moved out while I was preparing for what should have been the most romantic night of our lives. I hadn't seen her again until tonight. And fucking engaged. Probably to the same prick she was screwing around with behind my back."

Tired of using the glass, he drank straight from the bottle. What the hell. He was beyond caring.

"I never thought anything could hurt more until I saw her all gorgeous and fucking happy, and there I was attempting to drown myself in a platter of baby back ribs. I didn't think she could ever break my heart twice, but she managed it quite nicely tonight."

"I'm sorry," Kaz murmured.

The sincerity in those blue eyes raised Milo's ire. "Don't pity me. I may look pathetic right now, but come morning I *will* be fine."

He tilted his head back, mouth open, and poured more booze down his throat. The bottle was running dangerously low.

Then he slurred out, "There's no such thing as a happily ever after, Kaz. Be good to remember that."

"How can you be so sure?"

"Because mine just ripped out my heart and stomped on it with size eight stiletto Christian Louboutins." He slid out of his side of the booth and slipped in beside Kaz.

Beneath the scent of scotch, Kaz smelled of musk and spice. Of course. A masculine scent for such a masculine man.

Milo could never pull off that kind of cologne. He opted for cooler scents. His inhibitions had finally left the building when he leaned in and pressed his nose against the swath of skin above Kaz's shirt collar. The man didn't flinch away—a testament to his confidence.

Then he said, "Goes to show what happens when you let your guard down. Love will eat you alive and spit you out." Without thinking of the consequences of his actions, he snuggled closer against Kaz and rested his head on the other man's strong shoulder. "That's why, after what that bitch Celeste did, I promised myself I would never fall in love again. For an entire year, I buried myself in work and became Cassandra's executive assistant. I'm learning everything I can about how *Rebel* operates, making important contacts in the fashion industry, like Kenji, and preparing myself for the day I can take over."

"Sounds like a good plan," Kaz said. He shifted, settled his arm around Milo's shoulders, and pulled him in closer.

All Milo could think was how warm the man sitting beside him felt against his own body. No matter how hot under the collar he got from the massive amounts of tequila he'd been drinking, he couldn't get enough of the heat that emanated from Kaz.

To think the day started with him being so intimidated by this serious, eloquent, handsome-as-sin Japanese businessman. Now that they'd spent some time together and he'd bared his soul, there was nothing intimidating about him at all. In fact, beneath his stoic shell was a sex appeal Milo found quite attractive. He was drunk enough to admit that to himself. He'd been working around beautiful people long enough to appreciate high quality when he saw it.

"Have you ever considered being a model?" he murmured up at Kaz. "I'm pretty sure Brioni would hire you on the spot for any one of their catalogs."

Husky laughter reverberated from deep inside Kaz. The sound hit Milo in all the right places, and he lamented the layers of clothing that separated them.

"You, my friend, are sufficiently drunk."

CHAPTER FOUR
BED

LEANING HEAVILY against Kaz's solid and capable body, Milo let himself be steered toward the massive bed located against one wall of an equally massive room in the apartment that blew his mind. Granted, it was a mind addled by copious amounts of alcohol. Kaz had cut him off by the time he finished half the bottle, much to his annoyance.

"Where are we?" he slurred into Kaz's face.

Kaz didn't grimace or pull away. "My place."

A hiccup turned into a burp. "But why not my place?"

Kaz trudged onward, and Milo's legs dangled like useless spaghetti limbs. "I kept asking you the address, and you kept saying you don't remember."

"Oh yeah." A silly grin stretched across his face. "I have 'nesia."

"You mean amnesia." Kaz set him down on the bed.

"Yeah." He hiccupped again. "I'm not drunk enough."

"Oh, trust me, you're drunk enough," he said, nudging Milo to lie down.

He complied and stretched out on the side of the bed. The sheets were soft and cool beneath his overheated skin and smelled of Kaz—all man. All good. He sighed in contentment before he murmured, "Why did we leave the bar again?"

A chuckle reached his ears before the words. "When you suggested spending the rest of the night at karaoke, I decided it was time to pack it in. I may be Japanese, but I'm not *that* Japanese."

"Karaoke," Milo repeated, chuckling into a snort. "Funny word."

"Hai, hai."

He lay still as Kaz removed his shoes and socks. He wiggled his toes in pleasure. Then Kaz moved on to his jacket, which required Milo to sit up slightly. He groaned at being jostled and closed his eyes as the room spun.

"Not good." He rubbed his forehead.

"Are you going to be sick?"

He paused. Waited. When his stomach settled and no bile climbed his throat, he smiled.

"Nope. I'm good." He licked his lips. "I may be a bad drunk, but I don't puke."

"Just in case, I'm leaving a bucket beside the bed."

"Good to know."

The edge of the mattress dipped, which forced Milo to open his eyes. Kaz gazed down at him. He crossed one leg over the other and used one hand to ease Milo's tie off. Then he popped open the first two buttons of his shirt.

Despite his state of inebriation, or maybe because of it, Milo found Kaz undressing him incredibly sexy. He'd been with other men. One of those relationships was in college, before he met Celeste. An artist. It didn't last. The guy was too moody.

That night Milo wondered what it would be like to have those firm lips against his, how it would feel to be kissed by such a serious man. Yet how inappropriate would it be if he initiated anything?

Kaz didn't seem to mind when he sat next to him at the bar. He didn't even move away or seem uncomfortable. And from the way Kaz looked at him, with heat in those cool blue eyes, Milo could see something went on behind that stoic exterior. The question then became—was he brave enough to explore beyond the surface?

"What are you thinking?" Kaz asked softly.

It took Milo a second to realize Kaz had spoken in Japanese. Instead of replying, he reached up and ran the tip of his finger over the top edge of Kaz's lips. Kaz took Milo's hand and pressed a kiss against his palm. He might as well have taken Milo's cock in his mouth from the way his body reacted to that one point of contact.

28

"We're not doing this tonight," he whispered against Milo's palm, switching back to English.

"Why not? I know you want to," he said plainly.

Letting go of his hand, Kaz moved to stand. With speed someone drunk shouldn't have possessed, Milo grabbed his tie and pulled him down. The unexpected maneuver brought Kaz's lips to where Milo wanted them to be—against his own. Kaz barely kept from crushing him by bracing his hands on either side of Milo's body.

Taking advantage of the shock, Milo slipped his tongue between Kaz's teeth. He tasted the burned apple flavor of the scotch he'd favored all night and the Marlboro Reds he smoked. A moan climbed up his throat at the heady combination.

The sound seemed to wake Kaz from his shock, because he pushed up. But just as Milo was about to apologize for reading the signals wrong, he said, "You're not thinking straight right now."

"No." He shook his head. "But my life sucks at the moment, so why should it matter?"

"And you think sleeping with me will solve that?"

Milo thought about it. "No, but it will make me feel good. Don't you want to feel good? Even for just a night?"

A shudder went through Kaz. He closed his eyes and leaned his forehead against Milo's. "Not when it's something you can't freely decide on. When I take you, it will be when you're sober so you'll feel every inch of me sliding in and out of you. That's a promise."

Lightning-bolt quick, Kaz got up and walked out of his bedroom, leaving Milo stunned and a little more than turned on.

MILO LAY in bed—*Kaz's* bed—wider awake than when he'd been left alone. Kaz's words sobered him somewhat. Over and over he replayed what he said and imagined the heat of promise behind those eyes.

A man who was a complete stranger to him promised that he would take him, that when he did, he wanted Milo to be 100 percent present for it. A blush spread across his face at the mere thought of letting that man have his way. It wasn't often that he found himself this ready and willing.

His hand traveled down until his fingertips grazed the evident bulge behind the zipper of his pants. He groaned, needing some kind of release. It might have been hours since he'd been left alone. For all he knew, it could have been minutes. He had no concept of time in the semidarkness of the bedroom. Where could Kaz be?

The instant the question came to mind, Milo pictured his face— the raven-wing eyebrows, the firm lips, the chiseled jawline. His mouth watered. He hadn't even seen what the guy looked like naked, and there he was already lusting after him.

He swallowed and brought his hand to his lips. The taste of *his* mouth still lingered, and if Milo thought hard enough, he could still feel the kiss. He moved his other hand to his belt and unfastened it. He had to do something about his arousal or he wouldn't get any sleep.

Milo unbuttoned his pants and slid the zipper down. The unclasping of metal teeth seemed the loudest sound in that too-quiet room, but he didn't care as he eased his fingers into the waistband of his boxer briefs. Moisture met his touch as he squeezed the head of his cock. He ran his thumb over the slit, causing his hips to rise off the mattress.

To keep from moaning, he bit down on the knuckle of his forefinger. What would Kaz think if he walked in and found him fondling himself in his bed?

The thought of getting caught spurred him on. Let him get caught. Maybe it would lead to more.

In his mind he slowly undressed Kaz, imagining what that body would look like. Surely it would be toned. He seemed like the type to have great abs. Milo had seen his fair share from all the male-model shoots he'd supervised on Cassandra's behalf. If Kaz looked that good in a suit, he would definitely be hot out of it.

As the picture took shape, Milo closed his eyes, grasped the base of his erection, and began to rub up and down the shaft. He applied pressure as he reached the tip. His tongue flicked at the knuckle between his teeth. He conjured up the kiss again—the feel of those lips, the taste of him. He rubbed harder, faster, losing himself until every muscle liquified.

MILO WOKE up the next morning with the taste of something dead in his mouth. He rolled onto his side and his arm fell off the edge of the bed. The hangover came fast and furious, taking him for twelve rounds in the ring without allowing him to put his arms up to defend himself.

Gingerly, he rolled onto his back as a wave of nausea assailed him. He breathed long and deep through his mouth. The cool air around him helped immensely.

Once he was sure he wasn't going to puke, he opened his eyes— first one, then the other—to stare up at a ceiling not his own. The realization that he wasn't lying on his own bed pushed him to sit. Where the hell was he, and what the hell was he doing here?

He looked around to get his bearings but didn't recognize anything in the room—not the modern furnishings, not the massive windows to his left where the gray curtains were drawn, not the bank of mirrors to his right.

A stabbing pain began behind his eye, and he pushed the heel of his hand against it. The only things he recognized were his clothes hanging from a hook behind the closed door. His shoes were to the side, the ball of his socks in one.

If his clothes were on the other side of the room, that meant....

He lifted the sheet covering him and sighed in relief when he found himself still in his boxer briefs. Good. He didn't get crazy enough to get naked. The only thing he remembered was spilling his guts to Kaz at Santino and finding him incredibly—

He slapped a hand over his mouth.

No!

That couldn't be.

The idea of doing anything other than drink with Kazuhiko Yukifumi, the business partner of one of the most important up-and-coming designers debuting in the pages of *Rebel*... Cassandra would skewer his balls and cook them for dinner if she got wind of any inappropriate conduct between him and Kaz.

The fear for his life pushed down the hangover deep enough to allow Milo to get out of bed and dress. Once fully clothed he opened the door and peeked his head out. The vast empty living room and adjoining kitchen mirrored the modern furnishings of the bedroom in tones of gray, white, and black.

He breathed a sigh of relief and, as quietly as possible, made his way to the front door. From somewhere in the apartment, he heard Kaz's voice. He was speaking to someone, but since Milo couldn't hear the second voice, he assumed it was a phone conversation. Maybe he had an office? If that was so, he was occupied. Good.

Seeing his chance, he opened the door, slipped out, and made a run for it.

CHAPTER FIVE
BRUISE

MILO RESTED against the door of his two-bedroom apartment, eyes closed, feeling out the emptiness of the space. There was a bottle of aspirin with his name on it in the bathroom. He fought against the lingering effects of the nausea brought on by the cab driver swerving like a madman.

Thank goodness he didn't have to go in until the afternoon. In honor of Valentine's Day, Cassandra gave the entire office the morning off. It was the closest thing to being romantic she allowed herself to be.

When he finally regained enough strength to make it to the bathroom, he opened his eyes and raised his head just in time to catch a glimpse of a shirtless man in sweats with a messy mop of brown hair, a perpetual scruff on his jaw, and the greenest eyes known to man. He sauntered out from the right side of the apartment toward the common room and kitchen at the center. They should really make it illegal for hot men to wear sweats that hung low on their hips.

"Tommy," he said. "I didn't think you'd be back so soon."

Tomas Barcelona, his roommate and the current face of Hugo Boss, gave him the panty-melting grin that had made him a male model. "Shoot's done. I'll be in the city for Mercedes-Benz Fashion Week before I hit the runways of PFW. Plus, I'm sneaking in a job Cassandra wants me to do for *Rebel*."

And that, in a nutshell, was his schedule, which Milo would have known had he been less… distracted.

"The American Body Shoot," he said as his brain began to function again—not at optimal levels, but nothing a shower and lots of fluids couldn't fix.

He'd completely forgotten that their jobs meshed. Tommy was currently the top model at his agency, which kept him busy. Every designer who had a men's line wanted him to walk their runway. For Mercedes-Benz alone, he was walking for Armani, Hugo Boss, and Brioni.

The memory of how Kaz's lips felt on his made him stagger against the door for support and bring his hand up to touch his suddenly tingling mouth. Jesus. So all of it wasn't just a dream. Had he really hit on one of their clients?

"Oh God," he whispered into his hand. All the blood rushed from his face to congregate in the soles of his feet. How he was still standing escaped him.

"You look like shit," Tommy said. "No, you look like what comes out of shit."

Remembering he wasn't alone, he pushed away from the door and lurched forward. No point in hiding the cause of his current state from his friend.

"I ran into Celeste last night."

Tommy gave a long, low whistle. He placed his hands on his hips, further emphasizing the V of muscle that men and women alike lost their minds over. Kaz had one of those too.

Milo mentally slapped himself when Tommy asked, "And?"

"She's engaged."

"Whoa." He wiped a hand down his face. "On the same night she—"

"No… I don't know… maybe." Milo shook his head to clear the urge to find himself at the bottom of yet another tequila bottle. "Anyway, I spent the rest of the night at Santino."

"And you're just getting back now?" He moved closer. "You should have called me."

Milo shrugged off the hand Tommy rested on his shoulder. "I just need a couple aspirin and a nap. I'm fine." The skepticism on his roommate's chiseled features forced him to add, "Thanks for the concern. I really appreciate it."

Not that it mattered since he didn't know Tommy was back until this morning. Calling him wasn't an option.

"Judging from the way you look right now, you're still hung up on her." He crossed his arms and scowled.

The pose was magazine-spread ready. Sometimes it hurt to look at him.

Without hesitation, he pulled Tommy into a tight embrace. At the lowest point of his life, Tommy had been there. He ended the lease on his place and moved into the apartment they shared now.

He fed Milo when he forgot to eat because he was too consumed with grief to do more than stay in bed. He covered for him with Cassandra when he missed work. And he was the one who had convinced Milo there was life after Celeste.

"I should have come home earlier," Tommy whispered against his neck. "I should have been here yesterday, knowing what day it was."

"You were in Bulgaria shooting the Spring/Summer catalog for Hugo Boss."

The hard lines on Tommy's face softened when he pulled back so they could look each other in the eye. "My job is to worry about you and then report back to your mother."

"This tag team you have with her is creepy. You know that, right?"

"Cut me some slack, will you?" Tommy finally let him go and stepped back, grimacing. "No one can say no to the queen of the models. Your mother is an icon. Even the guys revere her. So when she asks you to look out for her precious son, you do it without question or you get blackballed."

An amused snort escaped Milo before he could think to suppress it. "Look, thanks for the concern, but I would really appreciate it if you'd leave this particular incident out of your weekly reports to Her Majesty." He ran his fingers through his ratty hair. He badly needed a shower. "She's already worried enough.

Worrying her more about something this insignificant may mess with her health." Yeah, he played the recovery card and wasn't ashamed of it if it got him what he wanted, which was Tommy scratching the back of his head and nodding somberly. "Good. Thanks."

As he turned on his heel to go in search of painkillers and a shower, Tommy said, "Wanna head into *Rebel* together?"

"Yeah. Sure."

"I'm thinking greasy Chinese food for lunch?"

"Perfect."

Milo headed toward his side of their place and straight into his bathroom. He leaned both hands on the sink and stared at himself in the mirror. Tommy was right. He looked like what shit crapped out.

Thank goodness for small miracles that he made his escape from Kaz's apartment before he saw him this way. Bags under his eyes. Overnight scruff—the unsexy kind. And chapped lips. Not to mention the hair.

Not that Milo ever planned on seeing the man again. He said he was Kenji's silent partner. Being at the shoot yesterday might be a one-time thing. At least he prayed it would be, because he didn't know what he would do or how he would react if they ran into each other. The reaction of his cock to the mere thought of seeing him was warning enough that he was stepping into dangerous territory.

He slapped his sallow cheeks with both hands to wake himself up further. He had no time to play around if he wanted to succeed Cassandra as editor in chief. He opened the medicine cabinet and grabbed the white aspirin bottle, popped two into his mouth, and threw his head back to dry swallow. Then he ran the shower.

While the water warmed, he stripped out of his clothes, placed the suit and shirt on a hanger for dry cleaning. He reached for the waistband of his boxer briefs, and the final memory he'd been avoiding since he got home returned with a vengeance. His hand on his dick, jerking himself off to the image of Kaz naked.

"Fuck."

Fed and feeling like a human again, Milo stepped out of the elevator with Tommy by his side. This time, no confetti rain greeted him. Damn if he didn't breathe a sigh of relief at that.

For the entire commute, he worried his bottom lip. He didn't know exactly how he felt about what he'd done. He definitely found Kaz unbelievably attractive, as much as he hated to admit it. But Milo wasn't about to derail his career for a man who could ruin him in the end.

No.

As long as he didn't think about Kaz, he could pretend he didn't exist, that what happened last night was nothing but a fever dream.

At the sight of Tommy, Kasey whipped her head up and beamed from behind reception. "Welcome back, Mr. Barcelona," she greeted in a sickeningly sweet voice.

Tommy leaned against the counter and spoke in that husky whisper he reserved for all women. "Hey, Kasey. Missed me?"

"You're looking particularly yummy today," Garret said, seeming to materialize out of thin air.

"Put your tongue back in your mouth, Garret," Milo admonished. "I swear you must have some kind of alarm that goes off the second Tommy enters the building."

Garret didn't even bother taking his eyes away from Tommy as he took in the distressed jeans, white T, and leather jacket Tommy wore. "I guess that tracking chip is working well."

Milo rolled his eyes. "Unlike you three flirts, I have work to do. Any messages, Kasey?"

It took him slapping the counter several times to get her to acknowledge his question.

"No messages. Cassandra isn't in yet," she said in an annoyed tone, as if giving Milo her undivided attention were a chore when it could be lavished on the perfect specimen of man-flesh standing before her.

"Thank you," he said, pursing his lips and shaking his head.

As she stuck her tongue out at him, he turned and made his way to his desk. A crystal vase loaded with pristine white calla lilies waited for him with a card stuck between the blooms.

"Kasey," he called out, not taking his gaze away from the arrangement. Could it be Valentine's Day leftovers? Ugh! Let the torture end already. "What the hell is this? For Cassandra?"

"Oh, I completely forgot," she said distractedly from her perch. "Those arrived for you this morning."

Who the hell would send him flowers?

He reached for the card and pulled it out of the plastic holder. It didn't have an envelope, so all he had to do was flip it open.

Inside the note, in a masculine scrawl, was the question *Did you think of me?*

CHAPTER SIX
BREATHTAKING

IT SNOWED all through Mercedes-Benz Fashion Week. Cold, miserable flakes fell from the sky to settle as gray slush on the ground. Milo frowned as he stared at the clump of the sooty white stuff by his feet.

It described his mood perfectly—gray, miserable slush. Or *grush* as he liked to think of it. He pulled his coat tighter around himself and shoved his gloved hands deeper into his pockets.

Ten days after Kaz note-bombed him, Milo's confusion persisted. What could have Kaz meant by the question? He wanted answers so badly that it left him in a half-daze.

Ten days of Milo startling every time the phone at his desk rang. Ten days of staring aimlessly at the elevator doors as if by magic, Kaz would walk through them. As if he would have anything to do on their floor other than meet with Cassandra, which Milo would know about since he handled her calendar and arranged her schedule. Ten days of worrying over nothing.

What was he hoping for, anyway?

His life wasn't some romantic comedy where he would get swept off his feet by a dashing man and they would ride together toward the sunset of their happily ever after. Like he said at Santino, there was no such thing as happily ever after. Love crushed. That was what it did best.

"Pull your head out of your ass, Milo, and get in the game," he said through chattering teeth. Enough distractions.

The only reason he stood outside the massive white tent erected for the House of Suzuki show was because Kaz would be inside. Then again, he did say he was a silent partner. That didn't mean he had to be at every show or major event. But this was Mercedes-Benz—*the* fashion event on their side of the planet.

If there was one affair he had to attend for business, it would be this one. And Kenji was his best friend. Not inviting Kaz would be like Tommy not inviting him to any of the shows he walked.

Cassandra was already inside, probably wondering where the hell he could be or chatting it up with Kenji. At these things, one could never be certain the kind of mood she would be in. Since she'd taken a liking to the up-and-coming designer, Cassandra stayed pretty mellow. Maybe Milo could call in sick?

"What the hell are you doing out here?" Garret called from the entrance of the tent. "I've been looking everywhere for you."

Milo closed his eyes and sent up a silent prayer for strength. What Garret said was code for "Cassandra has been looking everywhere for you." He fisted his trembling hands inside his coat pockets to steady them. He didn't know whether they shook from the cold or from his hesitation to come inside.

So what if Kaz was here? It didn't change a thing.

Milo had no time for him. His only mistake had been leading Kaz on—and he blamed that on the tequila. He'd been nursing newly opened wounds from seeing Celeste happily engaged and had his guard down.

The attention he was given that night drove away some of the gnawing loneliness he felt. Sue him for going a little too far. That didn't mean Kaz had any claim on him.

"Come on!" Garret whined. "I'm freezing my cute tush off."

Somehow, losing his job by running away didn't seem as bad as it had in that moment. He didn't work for the money. In fact, his trust fund ensured he didn't have to work a day in his life. But why run away from something he enjoyed doing? All for a guy who embodied sexual attraction?

He still woke up from dreams of Kaz's mouth on the most intimate part of him, so turned on that it physically hurt not to relieve himself of the tension. One man scared him. Why? What was so bad about seeing him again? Maybe he could act like nothing happened.

Taking a deep breath of the bracing winter air, he turned around and faced the massive white tent that was quickly filling with a *Who's Who* of the fashion industry. Kenji's show was the hottest ticket in town. From A-list actresses looking for their next award season gown to top magazine editors and fashion bloggers, everyone who was anyone was invited to this thing. He'd heard from the event coordinator that they had to turn people away because the venue wasn't big enough.

Garret's lips were blue by the time Milo made his way up the stairs toward the tent entrance. Considering his hair was currently green, the look clashed horribly. A woman with a clipboard spoke into the wireless headset she had on, relaying the news that all guests had been accounted for. The show would start in less than twenty minutes.

"I'm asking you this again," Garret said as he followed Milo into the chaotic excitement of the tent.

Rows and rows of black-cloth-covered seats were juxtaposed against the long white runway. At one end, the photographers and members of the press were gathered. Toward the middle front row sat the VIPs.

People were seated according to importance. Cassandra would sit dead center. Her opinion was all that mattered.

"Why were you outside in this weather? Don't tell me you plan on getting sick before Paris Fashion Week, because you might as well kill everyone at *Rebel* to save them from the wrath of Cassandra if that happens."

"I just needed some air," Milo said.

He tugged off his gloves with his teeth, stuffed them into his pocket, and then adjusted the seat that would be Cassandra's. He would be sitting opposite her rather than at her side, because she wanted a report from the other side of the catwalk... as if the dresses would magically transform from across the aisle.

Milo was happy to do it, since it sharpened his fashion instincts. He often imagined himself as an editor in chief when he sat at these shows. What would she think? How would she judge which was noteworthy and which was just plain unfashionable?

At the head of the runway, he climbed the steps and veered left toward a short corridor that led directly into backstage. If the front was an excited chaos of people, the back was a frantic energy of movement.

Blurs of color zipped past. The brushes of makeup artists flew in when touch-ups were needed. Half the models were still in hair, while the other half were getting into Kenji's elaborate creations. At least three assistants were needed per dress.

In that war zone, Kenji was as calm as a sand garden—with scissors in his hand, no less. The lavender-haired designer snipped at a stray thread, fussed over a hemline, and at times even helped the model into a dress. He was in complete control of his universe. His creations were already stunning backstage. Milo imagined them under the bright lights of the catwalk, and it took his breath away.

It was promising to be a magnificent show.

The pandemonium reminded him why he loved fashion so much. It took him back to the days when his mother still walked—the sight of people running around like chickens with their heads cut off, the stinging scent of hairspray, and the screech of a producer herding models to line up. The chaos surrounding him seemed even more frenetic than ever.

Galvanized by a renewed resolve to focus on what he *did* know—that industry people spent billions of dollars every year on this—he fearlessly joined the fray. Garret vanished in search of his own boss. They had lots to do, since Cassandra wanted pictures of this show in the next issue.

The layout department hated having to move things around when most of the book—the final mockup of the magazine— was already locked in. But it was seemingly reckless decisions like these that kept Cassandra at the top of her game. A feature about Kenji during Mercedes-Benz Fashion Week would sell magazines.

Like a homing beacon drew him to her, Milo found said editor in chief standing a safe distance away from the stampeding mix of assistants, models, photographers, and whoever else scored invites backstage.

That day she chose to wear one of Kenji's tamer creations—a black-and-cream hemp dress with raven feathers woven into the material to give it a purplish-green sheen. It was a bold move on her part, since it declared to the world that she supported the Japanese designer 100 percent.

Nearing her late forties and still stunning—even better-looking than many of the models half her age. With her signature sunglasses on to blunt the harsh runway lights, Cassandra sipped champagne from a flute, her arms crossed. Her silver hair was ironed flat and framed her face. The tight line of her mouth didn't fool him.

She might look stern, but she wasn't displeased at all. The slight pursing at the center of her lips said she liked what she was seeing. But no actual judgments could be made until after the dresses withstood the runway test. Sometimes, under those punishing lights, things changed. What looked good one moment could seem hideous on the catwalk the next.

He removed his coat and handed it to one of the assistants to put away. Then he approached Cassandra, squaring his shoulders as he did. The producer by the front announced ten minutes to the show. He crooked his arm toward her.

"Escort you to your seat?" he asked with a calm he hadn't possessed minutes earlier. He was as Zen as Kenji now, with an underlying excitement for the spectacle they were about to witness.

Cassandra huffed once as a sign of her annoyance, but she took his arm anyway. "I would have you know that the only reason you're alive right now is because I love your mother dearly and was there as you were pushing your way out of her vagina."

"Ew, TMI!" Milo blushed scarlet. He glanced around to check if anyone had heard her and only sighed in relief when it seemed like the coast was clear. "Why would you have to bring that up? In public no less!"

"Because you decided to leave me alone when you should be by my side." Without breaking stride, she placed her half-empty flute on the tray of a passing waiter. "You haven't been yourself lately. What's been bothering you?"

"Noth—"

"And before you think to lie to me and say 'nothing,' remember I am your godmother as well as your boss. Not only can I fire you, I can bitch slap you and not care about a potential lawsuit. Am I making myself clear?"

Suddenly Milo was ten years old again and experimenting on which lipstick shade matched his skin tone. He'd come to the conclusion that Lancôme's Pink Posy worked best, but not until he'd massacred most of the samples scattered among the makeup station at one of his mother's shows. It was Armani Prive, if he remembered correctly. Stella laughed it off while Cassandra spent hours talking the makeup director out of murdering him.

"I'm fine," he said. "I'm just sorting out some feelings."

"I heard about Celeste." She kissed him on the cheek when they reached her seat. "That bitch was a fool to break your heart. Too bad she doesn't work in fashion."

"Tuck your claws back in. She has her own life, and I have mine." He held her hand as she arranged herself daintily on the seat.

"What life?" She frowned without looking up at him as she busily kept the complicated skirt of her dress from wrinkling. It was a feat that she managed to sit down. "You spend more time at the office than anyone else. You don't take any vacation time." She wagged a finger at him when he opened his mouth to respond. "Traveling the world to attend Fashion Week doesn't count. When was the last time you went out with someone?"

Immediately he remembered Kaz sitting across from him, sipping wine while he ate ribs. *Damn it!* That didn't count as a date, regardless of what happened afterward.

Kaz ran into him coincidentally and shared his table because the place was packed. So what if they had drinks at Santino after? Or that Milo spent the night at his place and passed out from jerking off while thinking of him?

To distract himself from the invasion of unwanted thoughts, Milo kissed the back of Cassandra's hand. "Don't worry about me. My mother does that enough for the both of you. Now, you and I have work to do."

His boss waved him away and put on her fashion-professional face.

Milo made his way to his seat and settled in. He fished out his tablet from his breast pocket and cued up the lookbook Kenji's people had sent out. Those in attendance could tap on the dresses they liked and could even make purchases or reservations on the spot using the devices provided for them.

He was busy scrolling through the pictures when the lights dimmed. Kenji stepped onto the runway and into a spotlight and polite applause. He spoke into a mic as purple as his hair and explained the inspiration for the geometric designs of his clothes. Then he thanked everyone for coming and asked that they enjoy the show.

The second he disappeared, Japanese pop music was pumped in and a cartoon of falling cherry blossoms played against the white wall that separated the front from backstage. As the first model rounded the corner, Milo recognized who was sitting beside Cassandra.

Time stopped.

The model's commanding strut seemed to slow to a stroll.

The music dulled.

The temperature climbed.

All at once his senses became attuned to only one person. Everything else faded away.

"Kaz," he said under his breath as his heartbeat kicked up.

And as if he had heard him, a slow, sensual smile stretched across Kaz's usually firm lips.

CHAPTER SEVEN
BACKBONE

MILO CROSSED his legs to hide the evidence of his reaction to Kaz in a three-piece suit and red necktie. He stared at him the entire time instead of watching the show. He really shouldn't have worn the slim-fit pants that day. With all the control he could muster, he pushed down the urge to squirm under the sex-on-a-stick's gaze.

The glare of the runway lights seemed to heighten the intensity of Kaz's blue eyes, almost turning them molten. So serious. So hungry. So much want that called to the deepest desires Milo hid within himself.

Kaz looked like he wanted nothing more than to cross the white stripe separating them and peel every article of clothing constricting Milo's skin. Considering his current state of arousal, Milo might just allow Kaz to do whatever he damn well wanted. Even with this distance between them, the air was electric.

All manner of thoughts assailed Milo, from kissing to having Kaz's lips travel to other parts of his body. Ten days of staring at nothing but the damnable vase of long-stemmed white calla lilies did this to him. Every time he moved to throw the blooms away, his hands hesitated.

All he had to do was nudge the crystal off the edge of his table and it would fall into the wastebasket. But the custodian regularly reminded him that only paper waste was permitted in desk bins. All wet trash must be taken to the trash cans near the communal bathrooms. And that walk would take him through the entire office floor.

Those who came to Cassandra's office already asked about the floral arrangement. He fended off the curious with reminders of work or questions of what their purpose was in visiting their fearless leader. That usually shut them up. But he didn't need the rest of the staff gossiping about who they could be from.

Ten days later, at such an important event, where he should be paying attention, all Milo could do was not squirm in his seat. The chill in the air that surrounded him was meant to keep the bright lights cool, but it also served as a reminder of how damp the front of his boxer briefs had become. For some reason his attraction to Kaz was more potent now than when he was slobbering drunk. Gone was the blame he put on the tequila.

He should be ashamed of what he'd done that night and all the thoughts that resulted because of it, but he wasn't. A part of him fantasized about what it would be like to have Kaz take him. Kaz seemed like the type who needed to be in control of all aspects of his life, especially those that involved pleasing a lover.

Milo's mouth watered. He swallowed and admonished himself for being distracted. Yet no matter how hard he tried to concentrate on the models walking past him and the magnificent dresses they showcased, just beyond the raised platform sat Kaz, still staring at him, almost unblinking. And he didn't even try to hide the desire in his expression. When Cassandra leaned toward him to whisper into his ear, all Kaz would do was lean his head toward her slightly while he kept his gaze on Milo.

His lungs constricted painfully, and the collar of Milo's shirt choked the air he needed to keep from passing out. He wished the show would end so he could leave. But he knew escape was futile. Cassandra would expect him backstage for press interviews and the after-party.

If he disappeared, she would hound him for being preoccupied, and his mother would definitely hear about it. With his first-of-the-month brunch right around the corner, the last thing he needed was Stella grilling him about his current emotional state.

He damned Kaz over and over for making him this preoccupied. He missed the days when he could act cool and professional. One night had changed all that. He had to admit thinking about Kaz really messed him up.

His attention pushed Milo's meticulously ordered world off its axis. He had to get a grip on the situation or risk crumbling under the pressure of work. Cassandra expected nothing less than perfection from him. If he couldn't deliver, he might as well kiss being the next editor in chief goodbye. And that was unacceptable.

When the model in the finale dress finally turned the corner, Milo took his first real breath since he noticed Kaz sitting across from him. The thousand-crane dress was so stunning it captured the attention of the entire audience. The ombré effect from white at the bodice to the deepest crimson at the hem elicited gasps and murmurs of pleasure.

Kenji's triumph was palpable in the air. Even Kaz looked away to watch the model saunter to the end of the runway, pause for pictures, then turn and walk away like she owned the room. And in that dress, she really did.

A moment later the line of models cantered down the catwalk with Kenji trailing after them at the tail end, behind the finale dress. The model was all smiles as she held his hand. Then she presented him with a bouquet of orchids, and Kenji kissed her knuckles and took a bow.

The applause was redoubled with shouts for an encore, as if this were some rock concert. Milo had only experienced this kind of response a couple of times while working under Cassandra's tutelage. And each time, she'd taken those designers under her wing.

She could spot talent before anyone else. That was what Milo aspired to. He wanted to learn how to detect the potential in a designer—that spark of genius so rare in a world where innovation could be as subtle as the raising of a hemline.

As the press horde and select members of the audience made their way to the backstage area, Milo unfolded himself from his seat. As discreetly as he could, he adjusted the front of his pants. How he wanted his coat at that moment to cover everything, but wearing it indoors would just look plain weird, and he hadn't reached the eccentricity phase of his life yet.

The first fashion reporter shoved a microphone and camera in his face before he'd even made it all the way backstage. Plastering on a gracious smile, he systematically answered as many questions as he could.

Praising Kenji wasn't hard. The guy knew what he was doing with hemp, and no other designer came close. The fabric manipulation… blah, blah, blah. On and on the questions went, from one reporter to the next.

Bloggers were more creative in their inquiries. Many of them, Milo suspected, dreamed of a career in fashion as a designer or as someone who worked for a magazine. He recognized the gleam in their eyes.

With his mind in work mode, he wasn't paying attention to his surroundings when the last reporter left his side to find the next person to interview. A large hand curled around his arm. After a quick tug, he found himself in one of the dressing enclosures.

Usually, they were left open, since models weren't shy about getting naked. But before he could blink, the curtains were tugged shut and he was pushed against the opposite wall. He gasped at the mouth suddenly crushed against his.

His surprise immediately wore off when the spicy musk of Kaz's cologne invaded his senses. As if the smell had some sort of aphrodisiac in it, Milo's entire body burned. A superheated blush rushed over his skin, and his heartbeat kicked into overdrive. Without thinking, he parted his lips.

Kaz ran with the invitation and explored the inside of his mouth with unbridled passion. Their tongues tangled in a sensual dance that flooded Milo's senses with all the hot lust that had been clinging to him since he left Kaz's apartment. The man could kiss.

It was only when a hand moved from his arm to cup the straining bulge between his legs that Milo spiraled back to reality. He turned his head away from the kiss, but Kaz was relentless, nibbling along his jaw and then down his neck. Only Milo's shirt collar prevented him from going further.

"We shouldn't," Milo gasped, thrusting his hips into Kaz's hand as he rubbed his length through the fabric of his pants.

"When you were this hard, did you think of me?" Kaz asked in Japanese, whispering the word in his ear and then planting a hungry kiss against the sensitive shell and nipping the tender flesh.

"How did you know?"

"You had cum all over your chest when I checked in on you."

That explained why he only had his boxer briefs on the next morning.

Knowing Kaz saw him that way after he passed out from jerking off made Milo's body buck off the wall to rub deliciously against Kaz's solid form. It was like pushing up against brick with the heat of a radiator. The idea of skin-to-skin contact slayed him.

To have Kaz stripped naked? Those muscles pressed against the lean lines of his own? It was enough for him to lose himself.

"They'll hear us," he whispered, even as his erection strained, begging for release.

"Yet this part of you doesn't seem too worried about it." Kaz ran his fingers up Milo's length until he reached the tip. "I'm pretty sure this part is already soaked."

Try as he might, Milo couldn't stifle his gasp of pleasure. "I need...."

"Need what?" Kaz spoke into his ear again.

The resulting shivers running up and down Milo's body weakened his knees. But before he could fall, Kaz wrapped a powerful arm around his waist to keep him upright.

"Kaz, please," he heard himself beg.

"Please, what?"

Instead of responding with words, Milo reached between them and pulled down his zipper. The rasp of the metal seemed like the loudest sound between them, other than the pounding of his heart against the shrinking walls of his chest. Could everyone beyond the curtain wall hear them? Surely they were making enough noise.

The idea of having someone hear what they were doing turned Milo on so much he was sure he'd pass out.

Kaz freed Milo's straining cock from behind his boxers. "Tell me what you want."

Suddenly shy, all he could do was shake his head. The hand Kaz wrapped around his shaft paused in its delicious caress, and Milo's moan turned into a groan of pain. Kaz silenced it with a searing kiss that was sure to bruise his mouth.

"Tell me what you want," he said against Milo's parted lips.

"Please," Milo panted more desperately.

He pushed himself against the hand still on him, craving some sort of friction, but Kaz pulled away, denying Milo what he wanted. He bit down on the corner of his mouth.

"I know what you want, Milo," Kaz said, his voice a dark rumble. Then he switched to Japanese again. "Tell me what you want."

Nani ga hoshii? Oshienasai.

The sensuality of the language pushed him over the edge. He responded by pushing up to his toes so his lips were just below Kaz's ear.

Then he whispered in the other man's native language the words he was waiting to hear, "Make me come."

"As you wish."

Kaz grabbed him at the base of his member and began pumping in a slow rhythm that he gradually increased. Milo's panting turned into ragged breaths. Not enough air entered his lungs, making him light-headed. He held on to Kaz's shoulders to keep his balance as his legs grew weak.

With each pull of his dick, Milo let out a mewling moan. The sensation of climbing a cliff increased until it reached a painful peak that seemed to settle at the base of his spine. He brought his mouth to one of his hands and bit down to muffle the sounds escaping his throat.

"No," Kaz commanded. "Don't hurt yourself. Bring your mouth to mine."

Milo's last coherent act before he spilled himself between them was to press his lips against Kaz's. As promised, the man swallowed each and every moan that left him as he lost himself in the pleasure he'd been dreaming of for ten days.

Ten days of nothing but flowers and silence.

CHAPTER EIGHT
BULLSHIT

MILO'S BODY still shook from the aftermath of his release when he tucked himself back into his boxer briefs and zipped up. His legs refused to support his weight, so he maintained a leaning position against the flimsy tent wall behind him. One rip in the fabric and he would tumble backward into the frigid February weather. Probably land on the *grush* he had compared his feelings to earlier.

Every muscle in his body was relaxed. Closing his eyes meant he would fall asleep where he attempted to maintain standing. The things Kaz did to him—one touch, one kiss, the way his body reacted. If this escalated to sex—which was an eventuality because there was no refusing Kaz—the act just might kill him.

No doubt about it. Kaz knew what he was doing. Thoughts of him being with other men—or women—ate at Milo's confidence. No! He shouldn't go there. He had no claim over Kaz. This—whatever it was between them—was purely physical. He refused to think of it as anything else.

Because anything else would destroy the life he'd managed to cobble together after Celeste. Opening himself up that way again, making himself vulnerable, just wasn't survivable a second time around, even with the help of his family and friends. Keeping things physical was the most he could do and stay sane. Nothing more.

While Milo focused on getting his breathing back to what resembled normal, Kaz pulled out his pocket square and wiped off his fingers. He had covered the head of Milo's penis to keep from soiling their clothes. Oddly, he found Kaz cleaning himself of his come erotic. He stared blatantly, and the tip of his tongue might have darted across his bottom lip.

If he continued down this path, he would soon find the front of his pants tightening again. As much as he wanted round two, it wasn't the right time or place. He wanted his first time with Kaz to be on a bed—the massive one in his elegantly modern apartment—with sheets softer than warm butter. He imagined how being naked would feel against a thousand thread count.

So caught up was Milo in his fantasy that he hadn't heard Kaz speak until those blue eyes studied him intently once more.

"I'm sorry?" He blinked as he struggled to return his brain to the present.

Kaz's features shifted to the stoic mask he preferred. Gone was the lust-filled expression he'd treated Milo to just moments ago. The sudden shift took his breath away just as much as how sexy Kaz looked. Such a huge difference, yet Milo's attraction hadn't diminished a single iota.

"I will go out first," Kaz repeated, tucking the soiled handkerchief into his breast pocket. "Wait a few minutes. Then follow."

Milo's eyes widened when Kaz didn't wait for a response.

Without looking back, he pushed aside the flap and rejoined the party as though they hadn't just been doing something extremely lewd inside the dressing area. The bliss that took minutes to build was shattered in seconds.

In two sentences, Kaz made Milo feel cheap and used. He might have been the one who got off in the deal, but it shouldn't have been that way—at an after-party, no less.

Finally, his legs gave out. He slid down to the floor and shoved his fingers through his hair. How could this have happened? How could he have let Kaz take complete control of him?

He should have refused. He should have been stronger. Should have held him off. Because he let his dick do the thinking, he'd been cast aside like trash.

Hot rivulets of shame streamed down his face as he did his best to stifle the accompanying sobs with a trembling hand.

TWO DAYS after Milo pieced together his dignity and picked himself up off the floor of the House of Suzuki tent, he sat front row at the only show he was invited to that didn't involve work. He went to the Hugo Boss Spring/Summer collection in support of Tommy. Watching him strut his stuff down the catwalk in a stunning suit was a small price Milo would gladly pay over and over. If he walked away with two new suits, he called it a perk. He'd already spotted a light gray number that would look good on him for Paris Fashion Week.

He compartmentalized what happened with Kaz and refused to give the incident much thought. It was his way of coping—push down the upsetting event and move forward. Dwelling wouldn't do him any good.

Should he kick down the guy's door and demand answers? Not likely. Instead, he poured himself into work—his constant source of solace. Work never betrayed him. Work never left him feeling less of himself.

Throughout the show, he kept glancing at the seat beside him. It remained empty, which was a rare occurrence. The organizers would never allow a vacant seat—especially one in front. So it baffled Milo until about halfway through.

He'd been placing an order for another suit that caught his eye when someone settled in beside him. The warm thigh that pressed against his forced him to address the invasion of his personal space. But when he turned to politely ask the person to move, he was met with Kaz's handsome profile. A lump immediately formed in his throat.

"What are you doing here?" he choked out. His hands turned into tight fists on his lap. There was hardly any room in the packed tent, so he couldn't move away from the contact without hitting the person sitting next to him.

Unwilling to create a scene, he gritted his teeth against the tingles that crawled up the length of his leg and congregated at his crotch. *Holy hell.* This man turned him on beyond sane thought. He hated it—not because of his lack of control but for the accompanying spark of excitement.

Nonchalantly Kaz said, "I'm watching the rest of the show."

The guy didn't even look Milo's way when he spoke. "You're late. It's rude to be late."

"Couldn't be helped. My meeting ran long."

"I thought the Japanese were known for punctuality."

This got him a sidelong glance as cold as ice in the summer. He sucked in a breath and then resettled in his seat. *Fine.* Let Kaz be that way.

At the exact moment he needed a distraction from the delicious slice of mancake sitting beside him, Tommy made his second appearance on the catwalk. He wore a navy pinstriped suit with a check shirt—a bold move for Hugo Boss but definitely worth seeing. Tommy's scruff and his messy mop of hair made matching checks and stripes look good—businessman with an edge.

When Tommy made his turn at the end of the runway and walked back, he gave Milo a wink. It was a running joke between them.

The first time Milo saw Tommy walk a show, he'd made a comment about Tommy being sex on legs. Since then, whenever Milo sat at a show Tommy walked, he would give a wink and Milo would return with an air kiss.

This time a hand closed around Milo's thigh and squeezed hard enough to hurt. He turned his gaze away from the models to glare at Kaz. He wasn't looking at him, but the tic of muscle along his jaw betrayed his rising temper. It gave Milo a sense of personal satisfaction he hadn't felt in a while.

"Jealous?" he teased.

Sure, it was like poking a sleeping bear or annoying a lounging lion, but he hardly gave a damn. If he was able to put some expression on that usually stoic face, then he was all for it. Call it a win.

"Who is that man to you?" Kaz hissed in Japanese.

Milo let his satisfaction show by curling his lips upward. Smugness wrapped around him as he leaned back and crossed his arms. The death grip on his thigh didn't seem so bad anymore.

"What's it to you?" he asked back in English.

For the first time since he arrived, Kaz twisted in his seat to face Milo full on. The ice in his pale gaze melted. "I asked you a question, and I expect an answer."

His eyebrows shot up. "Has anyone ever told you that you revert to Nihongo when you're pissed?"

A corner of Kaz's lips quirked up, but not in a good way. "This isn't a game to me, Milo, and I won't treat it like one. Stop playing with me. Who is he?"

Despite his dry mouth, he managed to say, "Mr. Yukifumi, the model is my friend. I'm here today to support him."

"Then why did he wink at you?"

"You're being ridiculous."

"Am I?"

Enough. He didn't have to explain himself any further. Thankfully the show ended, so he stood up and made his way backstage—like Kaz had done two days earlier—and Milo kept going without looking back. *Let him feel jealous. Serves him right.*

When Milo was sure he was safely hidden from view, he bent over, rested his hands on his knees, and breathed. The air that didn't contain that intoxicating spicy musk helped him gather his scattered thoughts. Being near Kaz screwed up his common sense. He didn't know what to do with himself. It was something new. With Celeste, he was always composed and self-assured.

"Milo!" Tommy called from across the backstage area.

He stood up straight, forced a smile, and waved at Tommy, who was currently being helped out of thousands of dollars' worth of merchandise. The green-eyed mancandy waved him over, but before Milo could do anything, a hand wrapping around his arm, preventing him from moving.

"What are you doing?" Milo asked, facing him

"You and I need to talk," Kaz said, lips in a stern line.

"There's nothing wrong with me saying hello to my friend."

"Of course there is when your 'friend' looks are you like you're something edible."

"Hey!" came a shout from behind them. "What the hell do you think you're doing?"

Milo groaned.

Of course Tommy would come to his rescue. He turned around in time to catch Tommy grab a hold of Kaz's shoulder.

"Milo and I need to talk," Kaz said simply… calmly even.

"You are most certainly not going anywhere with him," Tommy answered back.

A crowd gathered around them. Tomorrow this fiasco would be plastered in every gossip rag out there. He saw the headlines already— Famous Editor In Chief's Executive Assistant Causes Trouble at Hugo Boss Show. Top Model Tomas Barcelona and Prominent Businessman Kazuhiko Yukifumi Fight it Out. Milo McLaren in Lovers' Spat.

The list of horrifying articles went on and on in Milo's head. What would his mother think when she found out about this? Or his father? A chill ran down his spine.

That last thought was what made him say, "Tommy, it's okay."

"What?" Tommy's eyebrows came up.

Milo gave him a lopsided grin. "Let me handle this."

"Are you sure?"

"He's sure," Kaz chimed in.

"Shizuka ni shite!" Milo barked.

Kaz grunted but said nothing else after the command to shut up. *Good.* The brute could follow orders. So he continued his attempt at defusing the bomb or at least minimizing the potential damage.

His reputation he could fix. But if Tommy started a fight here, with a guest of the show, it would mean career suicide. No one would book him again.

"It's okay," Milo pleaded, tipping his head toward the photographers still snapping pictures. "I'll handle this."

Hands on his hips, Tommy let out the breath and said, "You make sure to call me, you hear?"

"I'll see you at home."

Kaz didn't seem to like that bit, because he cursed under his breath in Nihongo.

"If you need me…." Tommy left the rest unsaid.

"Yeah." Milo nodded once, then said to the barbarian who was the cause of the scene, "You can let go of my arm now. I'll go with you willingly."

"Not a chance," Kaz said as he led the way out of there.

CHAPTER NINE
BREAKPOINT

KAZ OPENED the door to the waiting town car and stood aside, letting Milo climb in before he slipped in after. As he pulled the door shut, he gave the driver instructions in Japanese, and even before Milo could ask where they were going, they were already on their way.

The angry bull of a businessman yanked him forward by his slim necktie and crushed his mouth with a punishing kiss. Milo gasped at the shock of the sudden contact, and Kaz used that opportunity to take full control. He nipped, sucked, licked—punishing yet arousing at the same time.

Milo's brain shut down in seconds. Gone was the annoyance, the fear, the worry. All emotions vanished but for the lust bubbling beneath his skin.

He gave himself willingly to the kiss. Resistance was futile. Despite the nipping and bruising pressure, the hisses of pain quickly became moans of desire. Milo was a goner, and he knew it.

With his sensual lips, Kaz took complete ownership of him.

As if to keep himself from plunging into depths unknown while their tongues tangled, Milo grabbed on to the powerful shoulders looming over him. Kaz's strength became his anchor in the storm of his own making. His body craved more.

Unconsciously, he inched forward until he was enveloped by the raging heat coming from Kaz as he forced his way through the barriers Milo put up to protect himself. But just as Milo began to participate in the kiss, Kaz broke away and eased his bulk to the other side of the back seat. Never in Milo's life had he felt so bereft.

Realizing he'd closed his eyes, Milo opened them to see Kaz resting his chin on a tight fist and looking out onto the crowded sidewalk as they stopped at a light. Still a stoic mask, except for the slight crumpling of the space between his ebony eyebrows. Milo was baffled at the sudden walls that had come up between them. He was supposed to be the one annoyed.

Tugging at his suit jacket and necktie to resettle them into place, he finally arranged himself on his side of the back seat. Then he crossed both his arms and legs. Kaz wasn't the only one who was capable of putting up fences. Milo schooled his features until his reflection in the car window resembled someone he used to know, but inside he knew meeting Kaz had changed him, disturbed the peace he'd so carefully reconstructed.

"Where are you taking me?" he asked, not having caught what Kaz said to his driver earlier because he had spoken too fast.

It took a full minute, but the brute eventually responded with, "Dinner. We were interrupted the last time."

That surprised him more than everything else so far. "You're taking me out on a date?"

The look he got in response was matter-of-fact. "Yes."

"But I thought…." He didn't allow himself to finish the sentence or Kaz would certainly hear the disappointment in his tone.

Kaz snorted. "I'd like to get to know you before I fuck you. Is that so wrong?"

It seemed as though Kaz read his mind, which sent shivers down Milo's spine.

"I don't get you," Milo blurted out.

"I would think I'm very simple. I'm clearly attracted to you. What else is there to understand? My jealousy made me lose control and abduct you from a fashion show."

Milo's jaw dropped. There were so many revelations in that one spoken breath that his head reeled.

"You're attracted to me?"

"Isn't it obvious? Or do you need another demonstration?"

He lifted both hands to stall Kaz's move to lean toward him. "Tommy doesn't like me like that. We were just messing around. An inside joke. Nothing more."

Another snort, this time filled with derision. "I guess it's true when they say you don't see what's right in front of you. That man clearly has feelings for you. It was in his eyes."

"I don't believe you. Tommy doesn't see me that way."

"You don't have to believe what I'm saying for me to be right." Kaz returned to street watching. "But you're mine."

And the punches kept on coming. "What the hell does that mean, anyway? I'm yours? I am no one's property."

Kaz narrowed his blue gaze at him. "Your mind may not see it yet, but your body certainly thinks so."

A burning flush scattered all over Milo's skin, and the erection that pushed against the front of his pants definitely agreed.

As if the truth didn't affect him, Milo cleared his throat and said, "Is that why you're taking me to dinner?"

Kaz whispered his name reverently as he reached out and ran a fingertip along Milo's jaw. He felt the touch all the way to the most sensitive part of his body.

"There's no point in taking you when I can't have all of you. I'm a very patient man. I want you aching for me, for my touch. Then, just when you can't stand to be without it anymore, I will give you what you've been craving since the morning we met."

"You should, at least, let me return the favor," Milo muttered grudgingly, gripping his arms so hard he was sure to leave nail marks even with layers of clothing between his fingers and skin. His tongue craved the taste of Kaz. "I know you're just as hard for me as I am for you."

No harm in admitting the truth.

"No."

"Why?"

"Because when I come for the first time it will be inside you," he said as if he was stating a fact. "You can make it up to me all you want after that."

Kaz's words thrilled and scared Milo in equal measure. Here was a man who knew what he wanted and did everything he could to get it. He admired Kaz for it, respected him even. Would it be so bad to explore something more than the physical with him?

A WOMAN in a tight black dress led the way into the VIP area of one of the most exclusive restaurants in the city. Not even Cassandra could make last-minute reservations there. Dinners would always have to be scheduled far in advance and only for the best talent who graced the pages of *Rebel*.

Yet there was Kaz, a walk-in, striding to their table as if he owned the place. That alone told Milo more than he ever thought he would learn from Kaz himself. He had to be someone extremely important—not just the silent partner of the House of Suzuki.

"What did you say you did again?" Milo asked as a waiter unfolded the starched napkin across his lap with one expert flip of his wrist.

Kaz ignored him. He ordered wine and then asked, "Is there anything specific you would like to eat? A slab of ribs, maybe?"

A blush crossed from one cheekbone to the other. "Not funny."

"I apologize."

The sincerity in his tone helped Milo return his gaze to confirm. Yup, the guy was being sincere. No hint of humor in those startling blue eyes.

He appreciated that when he said, "Whatever you're having is fine."

Kaz rattled off an order of surf and turf, but it wasn't just any surf and turf. It involved the best cut of meat, lobster tail out of the shell, and scallops the size of Milo's fist—the surf and turf of kings.

When the restaurant staff finally left them alone, Kaz sat back and studied Milo through a hooded gaze.

"Imports and exports," he said in response to the earlier question.

"But what does that mean, exactly?" Milo took a sip of his water. Sparkling. He studied the glass with raised eyebrows. Of course.

"My company imports things and exports other things."

"Can you be any vaguer?"

Kaz's lips curled upward. "Yes."

And Milo believed him too. "Why not just tell me?"

He didn't bat an eyelash when he said, "I don't want to bore you with details about work. I'm here because I want to spend time with you. I would appreciate the same from you."

Like a dart landing on the center dot of the board, Kaz got Milo there.

So he changed the topic to something non-work-related. "Why the sudden cold shoulder at Kenji's after-party?"

The spark in those blue depths ignited something primal behind Kaz's self-assurance. "Who said I was giving you the cold shoulder?"

"The fact that you ignored me for the rest of the night?"

"I wanted to have you by my side the entire time," he said in such low, husky tones that his words touched places in Milo he didn't care to explore in such a public space. "But would you have wanted that? You had work to do. I wanted to respect that. I had already overstepped my bounds by having my way with you in that dressing area. The last thing I wanted was to interfere further with your night."

He was already interfering, but Milo didn't say that. He wouldn't have allowed Kaz to hover around him while he worked anyway. What did he expect? That they would leave the dressing area holding hands like some couple in love?

Milo silently admonished himself for the self-imposed emotional torture. Kaz wasn't being cold. He was being considerate. He should have seen that. Understood it.

"I'm such an idiot," he mumbled in Japanese, specifically using the word *baka* to describe himself.

Uncharacteristically, Kaz threw his head back and laughed. It transformed his face and made him look younger than he usually seemed. And infinitely sexier. Damn, the man just kept on getting hotter the longer they spent time together.

Then ringing cut off the deep, melodic sound. Kaz reached into his breast pocket and pulled out a phone. He frowned at the screen but then swiped his thumb to answer the call. He brought the receiver to his ear and listened.

Milo didn't know what to do. Should he leave and give Kaz some privacy? But a part of him wanted to listen in on the call and watch Kaz in action.

"I'll take care of it later," Kaz said. Then he did something Milo wasn't expecting—he turned off his phone and replaced it into his pocket.

"You didn't have to do that."

"I said I would be spending this time with you, and I'm making good on my word." Kaz sighed as the waiter finally returned with the wine he had ordered. "Work can wait."

Milo's feelings of being special were cut short when shrill ringing cut through the air again. Kaz's eyebrows came together as he fished out a second phone from the back pocket of his pants. He answered with a growled, "What?" and then listened again.

"I said I'll take care of it later," he said through clenched teeth. He turned off the second phone and tossed it onto the table.

"Are you sure? For them to call you on your second phone, it must mean it's something really important. I don't mind if you have to go."

Milo knew the drill well. He'd sat through many dinners where his father was called away because of business. He held no resentment, just regrets about missed opportunities to spend family time together.

"Not as important as this dinner with you." Kaz took a sip of his wine, but the scowl on his features never eased.

Touched, Milo brought his own glass to his lips and appreciated the fruity notes in the selection—sweet with a slightly bitter bite. It would go well with their order. He had just taken his second sip when Kaz's driver arrived at their table.

The man seemed to be even larger than Kaz, if that was possible. Milo only noticed because they didn't have the barrier of the front seat between them. What looked like the tattoo of a dragon's claw peeked out of the man's collar.

66

Out of respect, he removed the cap he wore to reveal a closely shaven head. Then he bowed low and apologized in Japanese, ending his sentence with the word *Waka-sama*. Milo's eyebrows rose.

The driver handed his boss another cell phone. The murder on Kaz's face was both scary and funny—a scowl so severe it could cut a person in half with a slight eyebrow twitch. It made such an intimidating man seem adorable. At least Milo thought so.

Well, maybe not so much.

His driver paled significantly, without losing his stone-cold composure.

Kaz took the phone that was handed to him. This time, he didn't wait to hear what was being said on the other end. Instead, he barked threats of dismemberment for interrupting his dinner, all in measured Japanese. The intent was clear in his words.

When he ended the call, he handed the phone back and pushed away from the table. Milo moved to do the same, but Kaz stopped him with a raised hand.

"Please, enjoy the dinner." His frown deepened when he told his driver to leave and that he would follow shortly. When they were alone again, Kaz added, "I wish I could stay."

He traced the line of Milo's jaw again, ending by tipping Milo's chin up with his fingertip. Milo looked up. The hot hunger he saw kindled some of his own. Kaz's gaze widened a fraction. Then he ran his thumb over Milo's lips.

Milo nipped at the pad, eliciting a groan from the standing man. "You're making this very difficult."

"Good," Milo whispered. "Now go. I have surf and turf coming, and I'd like to enjoy the meal without interruptions."

Without hesitation, Kaz gripped Milo's chin and placed a searing kiss on his lips.

CHAPTER TEN
BRUNCH

FIVE DAYS of nothing had passed since Kaz left Milo at the restaurant with two orders of surf and turf. He was beginning to think it was an emerging pattern between them. They would begin with a spark of something, then a whole lot of nothing. They couldn't even explore the possibilities.

All of their interactions were stolen moments and interrupted dinners. As relationships went, they were edging toward the land of Not Worth It. Too complicated. Too overwhelming. Too....

He sighed the instant Kaz's face materialized in his mind. That man. Those lips. Words weren't adequate to describe him. Not anymore, anyway. He was more fantasy than reality in Milo's life.

His relationship with Tommy, on the other hand... well, strained would be the best word to describe it. More his doing than his friend's. After the revelation from Kaz that Tommy liked him, it was all Milo could think about. Was it true? Surely not?

Tommy was a player. He had a lover in every country he visited. He had slept with every male model signed to his agency.

He was a manwhore and even switched to girls when he felt like he needed a "palate cleanser," as he called them. That alone was proof he didn't see Milo as more than a friend. Yet Kaz spoke so matter-of-factly that Milo couldn't let go of the nagging feeling that he might be telling the truth.

Then he admonished himself for his lack of focus on the most important issue—brunch with his mother. She was the only woman alive who could bring his ballbuster of a father to his knees.

On this beautiful first day of March, he sat across from her in a well-lit, classy café next to Straus Park.

Stella von Stein sliced primly into a grape. A fucking grape. The tines of her fork and the edge of her knife didn't make contact with the porcelain.

Then, as if it were the juiciest piece of porterhouse steak, she brought half the fruit to her mouth and chewed seven times, like her mother had taught her. Only then did she swallow. A fucking grape.

Milo knew exactly what was going on, but he refused to confirm it by speaking.

He figured he had until she polished off her fruit platter before it was considered polite to make a run for it. From the way she was cutting up the already sliced fruit into even smaller bite-size pieces, this was going to take a while. Held hostage by his own mother. He would much prefer Kaz torment him for hours with his tongue and make him beg for release.

Normally she was all smiles and sunshine. It was his own fault she sent icicles his way. She hadn't said a word since he arrived, other than a curt greeting and her food order. It made him shift uncomfortably in his seat.

The fact that she was prolonging the inevitable was the torture portion of the inquisition. But instead of a black robe and a white wig, his inquisitor preferred a white Prada day dress paired with Gucci pumps and heirloom pearls. Her perfume smelled of money—the classic Chanel No. 5. Its cloying Upper East Side scent wafted across the table to him.

Since it was the weekend, she let her hair down around her slim shoulders instead of the tight twist she preferred. The cascading strands made it hard to believe she had a son in his twenties. The supermodel in her prevailed. She put women half her age to shame.

The irony of Milo's current location wasn't lost on him either when his waffles and Canadian bacon arrived. He sat in a café near a park dedicated to a woman who refused to save herself as the *Titanic* sank so she could stay with her beloved husband. He was going straight to hell.

The papers had been merciless. He had practically predicted the headlines down to the letter. Adding Tommy to the mix just stoked the fire even more. And it seemed Kaz had been hiding the fact that he was some big shot businessman, not just some importer and exporter.

Sakura Industries was responsible for the shipping and handling of a majority of goods coming from East Asia into the whole of North and South America.

Not willing to break the frigid silence, Milo drenched his plate with maple syrup. Then, fork and knife in hand, he cut a square out of his waffle, topped it with bacon, and skewered the stack. Taking care not to drip on his blazer and shirt, he brought the first bite to his lips.

"I had lunch with Cassandra yesterday."

Milo dropped the fork and pushed the plate away. Here it was. The end.

"Stella, you have to believe me when I say what happened at the Hugo Boss show was unfortunate. I should have handled it better."

That was when she finally met his gaze with the same rich hazel irises he possessed. "You're not going to eat any more?"

"I'm suddenly not very hungry." He took a swig from his glass of cucumber water and rose petals.

"Milo von Stein-McLaren! I will not tolerate rudeness in my presence. I would like to think I raised you better than that."

She had. She actually had. All the guilt in the world congregated in his gut.

"I'm so sorry, Mom. I really am." He wasn't sure if he was apologizing for being rude or for the catastrophe at NY Fashion Week.

Stella returned to her fruit platter and swallowed a tangerine segment.

"As I was saying," she said. "I had lunch with Cassandra yesterday, and she filled me in."

He slumped back in his chair, no longer concerned about proper posture. A tension headache stirred at his temples.

"What did she say?"

"That you've been distracted." She slanted a glance his way when she slammed her point home. "That your work has been suffering because of it. Not to mention that debacle at the Hugo Boss show, dragging Tommy into it. Thank goodness we managed to play it off as a publicity stunt, since all of you were wearing suits from that brand as the pictures were taken."

"I had it handled before Tommy decided to be the hero!" Like an out-of-body experience, he saw how disrespectful he was being to his mother by raising his voice, but he couldn't help it.

"Milo!" she gasped as though he'd stabbed her. "You know it doesn't matter to me who you fall in love with, but there is a proper place for these things. Having that man drag you out of the show like that with all those photographers? What were you thinking?"

He shifted, exchanging one crossed leg for another. "It all happened so fast. And who said anything about being in love? Kaz… Mr. Yukifumi got it in his head that…."

Milo huffed, unable to properly explain himself. What the hell could he say? That Kaz had this personal claim on him, and Milo's interaction with Tommy while he walked the runway triggered some jealous impulsivity in Kaz?

"First of all, I'm not angry because you're with a man. After what Celeste did—" She bit her lower lip to stop herself. Then she breathed in deeply, exhaled slowly, and forced a smile. "I'm happy that you're moving on. But do you have to make a spectacle of yourself while doing it? Being on Page Six isn't good for your career; you've got to know that. And let's not even speak about what your father thinks. He's not happy, Milo."

All the hope of a relationship with Kaz? Gone. Shriveled up like a raisin in the sun.

"You're right." He shoved his fingers through his hair. She had to mention his father. "I should have known better. I should have been more careful. It's just…." He took a deep breath of his own. "Finding out about Celeste being engaged on the same night she'd dumped me pushed me to make impulsive decisions. I lost focus."

Stella reached across the table, took his hand, and gave it a reassuring squeeze only mothers knew how to give. "Milo, you know that I love you and only want what's best for you. I'm sorry that you had to find out about Celeste that way. And I'm sorry that it drove you to become vulnerable. I wish I could take all the pain away, baby, I really do."

The corners of his eyes stung. "I loved her so much. She was my world. And now she's someone else's." He'd lived with that truth for weeks, but it didn't hurt any less. "Then there's Kaz...." It didn't seem appropriate to stay formal when tears were about to win over his best efforts to keep them in. "There's something about him that makes me feel again. After a whole year of hopelessness, he excites me. He says I'm his, but I don't know what that means exactly. We have these moments where I think I'm going to die just by being near him, and then he disappears for long stretches and I'm left doubting if any of it was real."

A small smile softened her features when she let go of his hand to brush away his distress with the pad of her thumb. "Reminds me of your father and—"

His raised eyebrow cut her off, but not for long.

"You should have seen us dance around each other. He had his business, and I was flying around the world for photo shoots and shows. I considered it a miracle if we saw each other for more than a few hours a month." Then she sighed, and shivers ran up and down her body. "Oh, but those hours were the hottest—"

"Mom!" The image of his parents getting it on dried up the tears faster than a lakebed during drought season.

She threw her head back and laughed—a magical, melodic sound that never failed to put him at ease. "Oh, Milo, don't be such a prude. You wouldn't be here today if it weren't for one of those few hours between me and your father."

His heart spasmed at witnessing the fierce love that showed on her face. For some reason, their relationship worked despite the distance between them. Could it be the same for him and Kaz? Did he dare hope again?

"But this is different." He spoke the truth that needed to be said.

"How could it be?" She became serious again. "As long as you're being smart about it, there's nothing wrong with loving him."

"You keep saying *love* like it's already a foregone conclusion."

Stella brought her linen napkin to the corners of her mouth and dabbed. "You crazy boy. You're forgetting who raised you. Unlike Tommy, who screws his way around, you're the monogamous type. You don't entertain a relationship with just anyone. How many people have you been with in your life?"

He shifted in his seat. She had him there.

MILO STAGGERED into the apartment.

Brunch with Stella sapped all his energy. She gave him a stern warning about maintaining his reputation and being careful, and he sat through it like a seven-year-old being scolded for messing with a can of hairspray and a lighter.

He dropped his keys. He needed to make a decision about Kaz.

"My mother is an exhausting woman," he said as he sauntered into the living room to find Tommy in well-worn jeans and an artfully ripped T-shirt that cost hundreds of dollars. Good Lord, no wonder the camera loved him.

Tommy gestured to the boxes of Chinese food that were spread out on the coffee table and handed Milo a margarita.

"She made a fruit platter last three fucking hours. I thought I'd never get out of there without committing a murder-suicide." Milo took a grateful gulp, tilted his head up, and closed his eyes.

"That bad?"

"She made me go through every detail of this thing with Kaz. Who does that? I don't even know if it's worth pursuing. It's like so many people are involved."

Milo left out his mother's lunch with Cassandra. Tommy would put too much meaning into it and would surely worry more than he already did. Milo couldn't have that. He was fine. He could deal.

Then it hit him. This was the first time in days that he wasn't awkward around Tommy. *Huh.* Maybe he was just being paranoid. Tommy wasn't acting differently.

"If you're worried about the tabloids—"

"Don't remind me." Milo mock shuddered. "I'm sorry you got dragged into this mess."

"Hey, nothing a little General Foo's, more margaritas, a movie, and—"

"Chocolate-chip cookie-dough ice cream?" he interrupted hopefully.

Tommy treated him to a megawatt smile that put every A-list actor to shame. Milo sagged onto one of the barstools.

"Thank God for friends."

"That's what I'm here for."

"What's the movie?" Milo asked as he shoved an entire egg roll into his mouth and chewed merrily, feeling a hundred times better than when he arrived.

All was right in the world. He didn't have to decide what to do with Kaz right that second. He could enjoy the company of his friend before the whirlwind that was Paris Fashion Week.

"I got the feeling you might be bloodthirsty after brunch with the queen bee, so I got *Battle Royale*."

"A movie where delinquent teens are placed on an island and forced to kill each other until only one survives?" His eyebrows shot up. "You know me too well."

"The appropriate response is 'Thank you, Tommy. You're my savior. Your sexual prowess is unrivaled, and I will worship you for the rest of my days.'"

Milo laughed and choked on his margarita. He swiped at a stream that dribbled down his chin. "Make me a couple more of these and I'll consider sucking your dick in gratitude."

"That's more like it."

CHAPTER ELEVEN
BACCHANAL

LATER THAT night Milo adjusted the black domino mask that stretched across his eyes. He had reluctantly agreed to attend a party downtown with Tommy, who insisted Milo needed a night out. That he had been moping around the apartment when he wasn't at work.

Annoyed, and wanting to prove Tommy wrong, Milo put on his best tux and got into a hired town car.

According to Tommy, they were shutting down one of the hottest clubs for the night to accommodate the party—a masquerade. Not many people could do that. It would take a considerable amount of money. Which was why the invite was the hottest ticket in town.

Milo agreed out of curiosity. Because of his job, he attended countless parties, but nothing so secretive. This had a clandestine quality that attracted him. The invite was black with elaborate white calligraphy printed on the thinnest vellum he had ever seen.

"Stop fidgeting," Tommy murmured from beside him in the dark back seat of the car. He squeezed Milo's thigh.

Instead of calming down, Milo jolted at the touch. There was a certain intimacy that came from being surrounded by a blanket of inky shadow. It brought back images of his kiss with Kaz in a different back seat on a different night. The scent of him still haunted Milo. He craved Kaz's taste and the warmth of his mouth... and the touch of his tongue.

Not wanting to give his friend the wrong idea, Milo eased his thigh away and said, "I'm just excited. This is the first time I've ever gone to something like this."

Tommy snorted. "Surely you've gone to a masquerade party before."

"Yeah, but nothing like this. Look." He lifted the invitation despite the gloom. "It doesn't crumple. Isn't that the coolest thing?"

"You're such a little kid."

"A little kid who wants to know what this is made of, because I'm sure Cassandra would love to use it for invites to her events."

Tommy snatched the invitation away. "Tonight is about letting loose, not work."

Milo pouted and crossed his arms like a chastised five-year-old. "Well, sue me for wanting to be good at what I do."

"There's good and there's anal. All you think about is work." A heavy pause. "Or *that guy*."

His ears pricked at the insinuation. "*That guy* means nothing to me."

The lie slipped out against the proclamations of his brain to shut the hell up.

"Right."

Even in the darkness, he could see the silhouette of Tommy shaking his head. Milo squeezed his mouth shut. Thoughts of Kaz preoccupied him, of course. He didn't have his number. He had no way of contacting him. And he would rather die than use the *Rebel* database to search for contact info. All he knew was the guy's address, but like hell would he go there.

And if he did go, what then?

They were little more than strangers. Milo had spent an entire day researching Kaz. All the articles about him were puff pieces. He wasn't on any social media. No information floated around about his private life. Besides the tabloid stuff that included him and Tommy, there was absolutely nothing about Kazuhiko Yukifumi out there that didn't seem intentional. It was like the guy didn't exist.

In no time he slid back into Mopey Land. Tommy was right. He needed a night to forget about that mysterious and often infuriating man who had managed to worm his way into Milo's life.

His mother had been right too. He needed to tread with caution. It wasn't just his reputation on the line. There was Tommy's, his mother's, and his father's most of all.

Archibald McLaren was a very private, very important man. In fact, he might even know who Kaz was, but Milo refused to think that far. The last thing he would ever do was go to his father for information about a man he might be infatuated with. It was a passing fling, nothing more.

Just when he couldn't take being in his head any longer, the car eased to a stop. Tommy got out first and rounded the car to open Milo's door. Milo smiled in silent thanks as he stepped onto the curb. Then they both headed toward Diablo. The sexy-she-devil neon sign flashed red, welcoming patrons with a sly smile and a wave of her tail.

They approached a large black man wearing an impeccably tailored suit and a red demon half-mask. Tommy handed him the invite. The man took out a lighter and set a corner on fire. In seconds, the invitation burst into flames and vanished. Milo was as impressed as a kid attending his first magic show.

The big man stepped aside and waved them in. Tommy gave him a nod and led the way. Afraid of getting lost and totally not wanting to be alone, Milo trailed behind him closely. The double doors were opened by two women dressed in lingerie who took their coats and gestured for them to continue on down a red-lit corridor to another door.

"What exactly is this party again?" Milo whispered as he walked side by side with a grinning Tommy, who sported a jester's mask that covered the upper half of his face.

"You'll see." He winked as he opened the door.

Milo stepped onto a raised balcony that looked down at the main dance floor. His eyes widened. Naked men and women hung from silk canopies from the ceiling, performing contortions and acrobatic dances that seemed to defy gravity.

At one corner were metal poles where women in various stages of undress danced for seated men in tuxes and masks. At another corner were large divans where people were actually having sex while others watched—men and women alike, all holding champagne flutes.

The massive bar had bare men and women lying on the top so attendees could partake in body shots. Then there was the stage where another group of men and women stood. In front of each of them was an easel with a piece of paper and pen.

Milo turned toward Tommy and hissed, "You brought me to a sex party?"

"People here prefer to call it a bacchanal," Tommy said nonchalantly. He also took in the entire area with the assessing eye of someone who wasn't a stranger to these events.

"An orgy by any other name!" Milo balled his fingers into fists at his sides. "*This* after my mother told me to take care of my reputation. What if someone recognizes—"

Tommy interrupted him by tapping his mask. "That's what these are for. This is a private party. Why do you think the invitation is burned before you enter? Everyone here is on the same boat as you. No one will say anything. Complete anonymity. Think of it like being in Las Vegas."

"What happens in Vegas stays in Vegas," Milo murmured. His previous anger and indignation lost some of its steam. "Still, I can't say I'm comfortable with all this."

"You're free to leave," Tommy whispered into his ear. His hot breath sent tingles up and down Milo's body. "But I'm asking you not to. Have some fun tonight."

Taking a deep breath, Milo noticed a sweetness in the air that he hadn't when they first came in. "What's that smell?"

"Just something to keep everyone relaxed."

"Drugs."

"Oh, Milo…." Tommy *tsk*ed at him. "Don't be such a prude."

He bristled. That was the second time that day he'd been called a prude. He'd said yes to the party—granted, he didn't know the details at the time—so he would make the most of it. Chalk it up to personal experience.

"Come on." Tommy moved away from the banister. "Time for watching is finished. Let's join the party. There's an item I want to bid on."

"So that *is* a silent auction." Milo pointed indiscreetly at the stage.

"Best escorts in the business. A night with them can be mind-blowing."

Tommy wound his way through the crowd and headed straight for a significantly hung man to the left of the stage. He scanned the bids and added his own at the end. Then he made eye contact and winked.

"Is there anyone you like?" Tommy asked. "You should put in a bid… drain some of that tension you've been walking around with."

Milo's shoulders hitched up at the insinuation that he was sexually frustrated. But as he scanned the auction items, he couldn't see himself sleeping with any of them, regardless of their supposed talents in bed. There was only one person….

He shook his head the instant Kaz's face entered his mind.

"I think I'll pass," he said.

"Suit yourself." Tommy led them to the bar, where he pointed at the defined abs of the man stretched out before them. "Body shot?"

"Uhm…."

But before Milo could refuse, a shot of tequila was shoved into his hand. He was never one to turn down a free drink, so at the count of three, he threw back the liquid fire and licked salt off the man's hip. The guy smiled at him suggestively when Milo straightened.

A scarlet blush burned across Milo's face. Thank goodness for the mask covering the top half.

"Another one?" Tommy offered.

He waved both hands. "I think I'll need something to eat first. Don't want to get slobbering drunk too fast."

Tommy pointed at the buffet table lining one wall. Milo nodded and made his way to the spread, passing servers who wore leather straps and nothing else and partygoers already buckets into their alcohol and whatever else they were serving that night. Considering all the sex happening around him, he wanted his wits intact.

The chances of someone taking advantage of him were high, like astronomically, going by all the lewd glances being thrown his way. He figured if he stayed away from more booze and pills, he would be fine.

When he reached the table, the food seemed normal enough—rack of lamb, a whole roasted pig with an apple in its open mouth, bowls and bowls of cherries, for some reason. There were chocolate-covered strawberries, oysters on a bed of salt and ice, and shrimp cocktail. But just to be safe, he picked up a cube of cheese skewered on a colorful toothpick, popped it into his mouth, and dropped the used toothpick into a bowl set aside for them.

"Is that all you're having?" someone asked from behind him.

Milo whirled around to face a woman in a red sequined gown that looked painted on. A black feather mask covered most of her face except for her ruby lips, which were smirking at him. She reached for a stack of chocolates.

Her arms were covered in silk gloves past her elbows. She picked up one cube and traced the seam of Milo's mouth with it. He could already taste the sweetness of the confection without having it on his tongue.

"Open up," she purred.

Unable to refuse since it would mean opening his mouth anyway and shaking his head just seemed rude, Milo did as he was told. As soon as the cube landed on his tongue, the chocolate melted. He didn't even need to chew.

She hummed in pleasure. "Good?"

"Yes," he said.

She gave him her half-full champagne flute, and Milo took it gratefully and swallowed the rest of its contents in one swig. It might not have been the smartest decision to be taking a drink from the glass of a complete stranger, but the chocolate left a medicinal aftertaste that he wanted to get rid of. It was like drinking cough syrup, but sweeter.

Then, almost instantly, his heart began to pound and his skin burned from the inside. He staggered backward. The only reason he didn't fall was the buffet table, which he used for support. He covered his mouth with his other hand when his vision doubled and his breathing became ragged.

"What the hell did you give me?" he managed to say between pants.

The woman giggled. "You seemed like you needed to loosen up. It's one of the best aphrodisiacs on this table. Fast acting. From the looks of you, it's already working."

The moment she said *aphrodisiac*, Milo's cock hardened to the point of pain. He groaned. This was the last time he was trusting Tommy to take him anywhere.

Using what little strength he had left, he shoved the woman away and moved to the stairs. Instead of screaming, the woman actually laughed. Milo didn't bother looking back. He had to get out of there.

With each agonizing step, his heart leaped into his throat. Its beats were so strong it drowned out the music being piped into the party. Damn it. What was happening to him?

He staggered to the door and hurried as best he could down the hall to the entrance, leaning one shoulder against the wall the entire time to keep from falling over. He knew if he fell, he wouldn't be able to get up without someone relieving the strain between his legs.

At the double doors, he waved away the woman who scrambled to find his coat. He stumbled out of the club and breathed in the bracing night air. Winter still lingered despite the lack of snow, but the cold did little to alleviate the lava flowing through his veins. He hugged himself and bent over. So much pain. He thought he might lose his mind from it.

The bouncer whistled, and a cab stopped at the curb. The guy must have taken pity on him because he guided Milo to the waiting car. A single touch sent sparks all over Milo's body, but he gritted his teeth as the bouncer eased him into the back seat.

Then Milo rattled out an address off the top of his head. He prayed he'd make it there still in one piece as the car pulled into traffic.

CHAPTER TWELVE
BEG

THIRTY EXCRUCIATING minutes later, Milo found himself outside Kaz's apartment, breathing hard, skin overheating. Sweat soaked through his dress shirt, and all manner of icky feelings clung to him as he waited outside the building until the doorman was occupied and the woman at reception took her break.

He expected to get caught at every step. Slipping through the front doors. Sprinting to the elevator. Even inside the cab, he watched the security camera located at the corner of the ceiling, sure someone would be waiting for him at Kaz's floor to intercept him and call the cops. A night in jail for trespassing in his condition was the last thing he needed.

This wasn't how he saw things going with Kaz, but the moment the aphrodisiac hit, he couldn't think of anyone else who he wanted to help him. He needed relief from the growing ache inside. It was a hunger so fierce it begged for release.

Never in his life had he thought arousal to be painful, but his cock throbbed. His balls swelled. The muscles at the base of his spine twitched.

To say he hurt all over was a grievous understatement.

Yet, at Kaz's door, he hesitated. What was the plan? Ring the bell and ask him to fuck his brains out?

He was harder than he had ever been in his entire life. That damn chocolate the crazy lady had given him was working his hormones. His skin prickled and his blood boiled.

83

He was so aroused that even a gust of wind made him moan. Lust infected every cell of his body like a deadly virus, and the only cure was behind the door he was standing in front of.

Then the thought hit him—*What if Kaz wasn't home?*

It was enough to chill him to the bone, but he was in such exquisite pain that he couldn't take it any longer. His lungs were a furnace, and sweat crawled down the side of his face. He was feverish—all flushed cheeks and swollen lips.

It had crossed his mind to relieve himself, but he doubted his hand would be enough. His mind made up, he rang the doorbell.

A pleasant ring reverberated from within the apartment.

At first, the place sounded empty. He bit his lower lip and squirmed. Even that was enough to make his mouth water with desire.

Sending a silent prayer to whomever would listen, he brought his trembling finger to the doorbell again. *He has to be home. Please let him be home.*

Every inhalation brought cold air down his sensitive throat, but each exhalation was fire.

He rang again.

And a minute later. Still no answer.

He thumped his forehead against the wood just as the door opened. He stumbled forward, but powerful hands caught him. He whimpered.

"Milo?" Kaz asked in that voice made for the bedroom.

Ah, it sounded so good. Milo grabbed Kaz's suit lapels to keep himself from sliding to the floor. His knees had gone weak.

"What's the matter?"

"Help," Milo breathed out. "Help me… please…."

Eyes widening, Kaz asked, "What happened to you?"

"Tommy…." He swallowed. It was getting harder and harder to speak. His mouth was so dry. "He brought me to a sex party."

"Sex party?"

He shook his head and gripped Kaz's lapels until his knuckles turned white. "This woman made me eat something. A chocolate square."

84

When Kaz still didn't seem to understand what he was saying, he took the other man's hand and brought it to his painful erection. The mere contact was enough to make his hips buck.

"Please, Kaz. I need you."

Quicker than a lightning strike, all the concern left Kaz's features. His expression hardened, and his blue eyes turned to ice. He pulled Milo deeper into the apartment and closed the door.

"You went to a party with Tommy," he said, tone guttural and harsh.

"Yes," Milo breathed out, his throat raw, as if he had been screaming.

"And you were given an aphrodisiac."

He panted, close to tears.

"Are you sure this is what you want?"

"Your help is what I want."

Kaz stepped aside and let Milo in. He closed the door then said, "Follow me."

Milo did as he was told despite the pain between his legs. Kaz strode into his office and pointed at the clear space at the center of the room.

"Wait here."

Then he left Milo standing at the center of the room while he made his way behind his desk.

Methodically, Kaz began clearing clutter. He stacked papers and placed them on a tray at one side. Then he closed his laptop and placed it on top of the papers.

When the desk had been cleared, he sat on his swivel chair, tented his fingers, and watched Milo, a quivering mess of pent-up desire.

"Kaz—"

"Take off your clothes," he interrupted in a soft, deliberate tone.

"What?" He blinked.

"Fuku o zenbu nuge," he repeated in Japanese, which gave the command more weight.

"Shouldn't we be in your bedroom?" He hugged himself as a shield against the cold stare coming from across the office.

"For this?" Kaz shook his head. "You got yourself into this mess, and you want me to help you, right?"

Milo nodded in defeat. He saw where this was going. Kaz wasn't going to give him relief in bed. This was his fault for going to that party, for not being careful enough.

He was asking for help, and the only way Kaz would participate was if he did what was asked. So he shrugged off his jacket and tugged off his bow tie. When he reached for the domino mask, Kaz interrupted him again.

"Masuku wa hazushinaide," he said.

Milo dropped his hand from the mask. So it was staying on. Okay.

He moved on to his shirt, which was soaked with sweat. Yet, bare-chested, the cool air in the room wasn't enough to alleviate the fire inside.

Shaking, he toed off his shoes and teetered as he removed his socks. All the discarded clothing pooled around him. At his belt, he paused.

"What's wrong?" Kaz asked, switching back to English.

"What are you planning to do to me?"

"From where I'm sitting, you're not in any position to ask."

Milo gritted his teeth. "I thought—"

"Thought what?" Kaz cut him off. "That I would take you to my room and fuck you until the drug wore off?" He shook his head slowly, deliberately. "I told you, the first time I take you is when you're aware of every inch of me entering your body. I won't have anything interfere with that. Nothing." He scowled. "Now, take off the rest of your clothes. I want you naked."

"This is bullshit. If you're not going to help me, then I might as well go elsewhere," Milo threatened with the last of his strength. He couldn't make it to the door even if he wanted to.

"Who said I wouldn't help you?" Kaz's stiff posture softened slightly. "The sooner you're naked, the faster you'll feel better."

At the end of his rope, Milo took a leap of faith. He unbuckled his belt and unfastened his pants, taking his time with the zipper. The front of his boxers beneath was already damp. The head of his cock was already peeking out of the waistband, he was so hard.

He let the pants drop and stepped out of them. His boxers soon followed. Kaz inhaled sharply when Milo straightened. Naked except for the mask, he stood in front of the man he desired. It was only then that he noticed the floor-to-ceiling windows. He immediately covered himself.

"No!" Kaz barked. The harshness in his tone returned. "Hands at your sides."

"But the windows." Milo trembled.

A part of him liked that no curtains covered the glass. Liked that they could have an audience somewhere in the dark night. The excitement warred with his sense of propriety.

"Come here." Kaz gestured for him.

Unadulterated lust was evident in his voice. Milo took pleasure in it as he reluctantly dropped his arms to his sides and took tentative steps forward. Kaz pushed back his chair to make room for him.

When Milo was standing between the desk and Kaz, he asked, "What?"

Kaz didn't reply right away. It became obvious that his eyes were too busy feasting on his naked flesh.

Milo wasn't muscular the way Kaz was. He exercised to stay healthy, not to cultivate muscle definition, but he was still proud of his physical form. He knew he was attractive, and based on the way Kaz's eyes roamed his body like a predator, he liked what he saw.

"*Kirei*," Kaz finally murmured.

Unable to help himself after being called beautiful in reverent tones by such a painfully proud and powerfully handsome man, Milo began to touch himself. Leaning back against the desk, he traced the edges of his lips before he ran his fingers down his neck to his chest. With one hand, he reached downward until he reached his erection.

The other he used to tweak his sensitive nipple. The tiny bud was already erect when he removed his clothes. It grew harder with each swipe of his fingers. When he used his thumb to circle it, his back arched forward. He bit down on the corner of his lip in pleasure.

Kaz's stare intensified. He hadn't said anything, but he didn't have to. The heat in his gaze said everything Milo needed to know as he stroked the length of his cock. He paused at the tip, sliding his thumb over the slit, spreading the bead of moisture that came from it all over the head.

"Keep watching me," Milo begged when he resumed pumping. "Kaz, just keep watching me." He licked his lips as he moved his hand to his other nipple. It was just as sensitive.

Kaz leaned back in his seat and tented his fingers once again. He crossed his legs and watched.

Even in his stillness, Kaz seemed to match the lust raging through Milo's body as he fondled himself. He spread his legs wider, not self-conscious at all in his wanton display. With each stroke, he felt himself climbing closer to his release. He alternated between pants and moans, never taking his gaze away from Kaz, who remained an impassive audience except for the molten need in his blue eyes. His self-control heightened Milo's hunger, and he rubbed harder, craving the friction he needed to come.

Just as he reached his limit, Kaz's lips quirked upward. That small shift in expression sent Milo over the edge. He came more intensely than he expected. Head thrown back, he cried out and spilled his seed.

Every muscle seemed to tremble, wound tight like bowstrings. But despite that, he was still hard in his hand.

Breathless, Milo lifted his head. Kaz hadn't moved from his seat, hadn't even shifted positions. He must have a will of iron not to show any emotion after what Milo had done.

"It's not enough," he admitted, pleaded.

"Sit on the desk," Kaz said.

Without question, Milo complied and took a seat until his legs dangled off the edge. He leaned back on his hands, unashamed of the evidence of his release covering his stomach and chest.

Let him see. Let him look his fill. Milo took power from it.

Kaz finally shifted in his seat and uncrossed his legs. The obvious bulge between his legs pleased Milo. So he wasn't impervious after all. He inched the chair forward until he was within touching distance.

"Pull your legs up until your feet are on the desk," Kaz instructed.

Milo did as he was asked.

"Spread your legs."

He did.

"Wider."

"Spread them the way you want them," he said, daring Kaz to touch him.

And touch Milo he did. He placed his large hands against the inside of Milo's thighs and parted his legs until he was fully exposed. He dropped his gaze to Milo's still-straining erection.

"Look at you," he murmured. He ran the tip of his forefinger across the slit, spreading the opaque bead over the head. "Just came and already itching for more."

Milo bit back a moan. Kaz hadn't done anything more than that little caress, and already Milo was about to lose it. What the hell was Kaz's power over him? Even without the help of an aphrodisiac, Milo ached for him.

Then Kaz used the same finger to trace along the underside of his penis, following the vein, causing the member to harden further. He curled one hand around the base and lightly squeezed. This time, the moan left Milo's throat. He no longer had the strength to hold back.

"*Onegai*," he begged.

"Please what?" Kaz ran the tip of his tongue down the length of Milo's inner thigh. Then, keeping his tongue flat, he started at the underside of Milo's balls and licked his way up to the tip of the head.

Milo grabbed a fistful of Kaz's hair. "Please, Kaz, *please*. I need you."

Taking pity on him—or perverse pleasure in his pain, Milo had no idea—Kaz gave the tip a quick kiss and then swirled his tongue around the underside of the head and took it into his mouth. He sucked so hard, Milo cried out. He had to let go of Kaz's hair just so he could support himself with both hands on the desk or he was sure he would fall.

"Kaz," he gasped out. "Your mouth, it's so hot."

Kaz growled as he took in more of Milo's length. Then he moved his mouth up and down Milo's shaft, humming as he went. It sent spine-tingling sensations all over Milo's body. It was all he could do not to buck his hips off the desk.

"Fuck, yes," he said. The effects of the aphrodisiac heightened all his senses, and he felt every touch a hundredfold. Even the smooth surface of the desk beneath his ass gave him pleasure.

Kaz released his cock with an audible pop, only to lick the underside from base to tip. The roughness of his tongue made Milo see spots.

"Look at you." Kaz kissed the tip again. "Trembling so much you might fall off my desk. Do I make you feel that good?"

"Isn't it obvious?" Milo glared down at him.

Instead of responding, Kaz pushed his fingers between Milo's lips.

Understanding what Kaz wanted, Milo sucked on the digits the way Kaz did to his dick. When his fingers were sufficiently lubricated, Kaz pulled them out of Milo's mouth and brought them to his opening. He circled the puckered rosette and then inserted one long finger. Milo gasped, the walls of his throat closing, preventing any air from leaving his lungs.

Covering his mouth with the back of his hand, Milo said, "So good."

He yelped when Kaz curled his finger and grazed his sweet spot. It made him light-headed, almost drunk.

"So tight," Kaz murmured. "Your walls are squeezing me. I can't wait to push my cock into you, Milo. To feel your warmth. To feel you milking me until I can't hold back anymore."

If he thought he was hard when Kaz went down on him, he wasn't prepared for the insertion of a second finger. His dick jerked and turned to steel.

"Kaz, please."

"What do you want, Milo?" he asked while he continued pumping his fingers in and out, twisting as he went. "Tell me what you want."

"Make me come," he said against the back of his hand. "Onegai."

Without another word, Kaz returned his mouth to Milo's waiting member. He set the pace with a few slow, deep bobs of his head, and then every time he pushed his fingers in, he sucked. Milo lost his mind. It felt so good to be touched… by Kaz.

Then Kaz moved his other hand to Milo's balls. He caressed the heavy sac and then gave them a sharp tug. In combination with the curling of his fingers, it sent Milo over the edge. He came so hard, his vision tunneled. His heels rose off the table, and his toes curled. Unable to support his body weight with his hands any longer, he fell back and lay flat on the desk.

Spent and exhausted, his labored breathing and his erratic heartbeat were the only sounds he heard. The rhythm quickly lulled him into a dreamless sleep.

CHAPTER THIRTEEN
BREAKFAST

THE TANTALIZING scent of freshly brewed coffee woke Milo slowly. He lay on his stomach, a pillow hugged against him as he took tentative sniffs of the air. The sound of something frying coaxed him further from sleep. He stretched.

Muscles he hadn't used in a while twitched, but it was a good kind of ache, the kind that brought a smile to his face. Feelings of satisfaction and relaxation that could only come from a bone-jarring orgasm washed over him as he pushed up to sit cross-legged on the bed. The sheets pooled around his lap as he rubbed the rest of the dream haze from his tired eyes.

He sighed and ran his fingers through his hair. The strands stuck out in several places. He had never come that hard before, but good luck getting him to admit that Kaz had anything to do with it. They didn't even go all the way. Would he survive it if they did?

He flattened his palm against his racing heart. The anticipation alone might kill him, yet he knew he was willing.

Nothing would keep him from having Kaz inside him. It was fate. It was inevitable. No use denying it.

How he felt for the man, on the other hand, was an entirely different story. He still wasn't sure. He didn't know him well enough. But he'd heard stories about strangers who fell in love at first sight. Was this something like that?

He slapped his cheeks. Good God, he hoped not. That would be way too cheesy. And—the thought gave him pause—no matter what he might feel, it didn't mean Kaz felt the same.

The night before was proof that he was attracted to him physically, but sex does not a relationship make. Milo didn't want that. If he was in it, he wanted to be in it all the way.

"Are you going to stay in bed all day?" Kaz asked from somewhere outside the room.

No use hiding. He suspected if he didn't move, Kaz would come in and get him. To save himself from being treated like a spoiled child, he inched out of bed.

The goose bumps rising on his skin from the room's temperature forced him to look down. Of course he was naked. He shook his head and searched for clothes.

His eyes landed on the dresser. On top was a folded shirt and boxers. Nothing else.

Sighing in defeat, Milo pulled on the boxers, which were a size too big, and shrugged on the shirt that reached all the way to his thighs and almost covered the boxers completely. Out of sheer curiosity, he lifted the collar and sniffed. Traces of Kaz's spicy musk lingered on the fabric. He committed the scent to memory for nights when he was alone.

"Where are my—" he began as he left the bedroom on his way to the kitchen. He spotted Kaz, shirtsleeves rolled up to his elbows, tie thrown over one shoulder, standing by the stove.

His mouth watered for two different reasons. First because Kaz looked hot and in control while cooking. Second because of what he was cooking.

Milo swallowed and said, "You're making me *tamagoyaki*?"

His insides melted as Kaz expertly rolled the egg omelet in the traditional Japanese rectangular pan using wooden chopsticks.

"There's also *natto*, *nori*, broiled *aji*—"

"Steamed rice, miso soup, and *tsukemono*," he finished in awe. "You made me a Japanese breakfast?"

He scanned the dining table, where bowls of rice sat among bowls of soup and plates of dried horse mackerel and an assortment of pickled vegetables, including his favorite—pickled ume plums, commonly known as *umeboshi*.

His heart swelled to five times its size. He was afraid it would burst out of his chest from joy. Unexpectedly, what did burst out of him were tears. They welled up fast and ran down his face to drip off his chin.

Kaz pursed his lips. "If you're going to cry, you might as well do it while eating. You need to get rid of the last traces of the aphrodisiac you took last night." He pointed at the table while he prepared the tamagoyaki for slicing on a cutting board.

Sniffing and wiping his watery eyes with the back of his hand, Milo approached the perfectly set table. He hadn't seen a breakfast like it since Tokyo, and it brought back painful memories, but the fact that Kaz was the one who prepared this meal for him blunted the pain significantly. He wasn't usually so emotional. Maybe it was a side effect of the aphrodisiac.

He couldn't deny that Kaz preparing him breakfast was the sweetest thing anyone had done for him in a long time. A fresh wave of emotion came over him as he pulled out a chair and sat down. He picked up the chopsticks and murmured "*itadakimasu*," which was the traditional phrase said before eating.

Then he reached for the bowl of rice, seasoned it with soy sauce, and topped it with the fermented soybeans. But before he could take his first bite, a yellow rectangle of rolled egg was placed on top of the *natto*. He looked up to see a concerned expression on Kaz's face. His dark eyebrows were together, and a prominent frown marred his good looks. More tears came.

Kaz rolled his perfect blue eyes and sighed. "Stop crying or...."

Then, as if making up his mind, he took a seat and pulled Milo onto his lap.

Milo yelped in surprise, almost spilling his bowl of rice and natto, but he didn't protest. The second he was enveloped by Kaz's scent, he settled immediately and rested the side of his head against Kaz's strong shoulder.

Kaz took the bowl and chopsticks from his hands and used the chopsticks to pick up the *tamagoyaki*. Milo obliged by parting his lips and taking the yellow brick of goodness into his mouth. He chewed thoughtfully, finding it fluffy and sweet, just the way he liked it.

"Nakanaide kudasai," Kaz murmured against the top of Milo's head.

In Japanese, the request for him to stop crying sounded so much sweeter, which only caused more of the waterworks.

"I can't," he said between hics and sniffs. "This... no one has ever done something like this for me."

Kaz tilted Milo's chin up and placed a kiss on his lips. When Milo moved to deepen the kiss, Kaz pulled back. It wasn't that kind of contact. A part of Milo knew it, so he didn't protest, even though he wanted to take things further.

"There's nothing I wouldn't do for you," Kaz whispered against his mouth.

Milo's heart jumped. "But you keep disappearing."

Kaz shook his head, amusement in his gaze. "I'm always right here."

"But I want more than just the occasional encounter. I don't even have your number."

This time, Kaz laughed. The sound reverberated from his chest. It was masculine and reached into places Milo thought had been dead since Celeste dumped him without mercy. It comforted him immensely and dried the tears he couldn't seem to control.

When Kaz regained his composure, he said, "If you scroll through your contacts, you'll find my number there."

"What?" His eyes widened. "How?"

"The first night you spent here, I programmed my number into your phone. Are you honestly telling me you haven't checked? Between you passing out every time I make you come and this, I have to say I'm crushed. I don't think my ego can recover."

Milo smacked Kaz's chest at the mock devastation. He wasn't sure if he blushed because Kaz was making fun of him or because he hadn't thought to check his phone. He was a call away the whole time?

"But how should I know!" he protested. "It's not like I scroll my contacts hoping your number would magically be there. And why haven't you called me?"

That was when the seriousness returned.

"Because I was afraid that if I did, you and I wouldn't get any work done." He rested his forehead against Milo's. "You do things to me, Milo. I'm usually proud of my control over my emotions, but when I'm with you, I unravel. Last night...."

"You seemed in complete control to me." Milo touched his cheek, loving how smooth it felt beneath his fingertips.

"If you only knew," Kaz whispered as though he didn't want anyone to know about his secret weaknesses. "If I could keep you by my side all the time, I would. But I don't want you resenting me or pushing me away, so I give you space. Whenever I feel like I can't take it anymore, I come to you."

Milo gasped as the truth of his words hit home. "Mercedes-Benz Fashion Week, the House of Suzuki and Hugo Boss shows."

Kaz nodded, rubbing their foreheads together. "Then last night you came here all hot and bothered. When you told me about the party, it was all I could do not to leave and murder that son of a bitch you call a friend."

"It wasn't his fault. I agreed to go to the party." He shrugged. "Granted, I didn't know it was a sex party until I got there."

A low growl emanated from Kaz. Milo moved his hand from Kaz's cheek to the back of his neck and squeezed away the mounting tension there. When he seemed to relax again, Milo continued.

"To be honest, I can't say I regret last night. Sure, being drugged sucked. But having you touch me...." He pulled back so he could look into Kaz's eyes. "You make me feel things I haven't felt for anyone before, Kazuhiko."

Desire sparked within those blue depths. The tip of Milo's tongue darted across his lower lip, which Kaz followed with his gaze. This time, when Kaz bent down and crushed their mouths together, he explored with wanton abandon.

A moan came out of Milo without hesitation. He tasted the coffee Kaz had been drinking. The bitterness mixed with the sweetness of his tongue sent sensations straight to his groin. Was this it? Was this the moment when he would get what he wanted most from Kaz?

But as though Kaz read the turn his thoughts had taken, Kaz broke the contact and rested his forehead against Milo's. Their breaths mingled, both clearly affected by that one kiss. Milo squirmed when he felt the bulge pressing against his hip.

"We can't," Kaz said, but his tone rang false.

"And why not?" Milo cupped Kaz's face with both hands.

"You have work. I have an important meeting. And this is not how I planned it."

The sincerity he tried to add to his husky tone made Milo chuckle. "Well, if that's the case, then you could at least let me return the favor." Without waiting for a response, Milo dropped to the floor and unzipped Kaz's pants. When Milo released his cock from behind the boxers keeping it prisoner, he gasped. "You're big."

"Milo," Kaz warned, glaring down at him.

He gave Kaz a winning smile and then put all his attention on the most important part of him at that moment. He purred and bypassed the throbbing cock on his descent. He cupped Kaz's balls and weighed them in his hand as Kaz sagged against the chair and groaned, his pupils dilating.

Milo licked his bottom lip in appreciation. Gone was the glaring guy, replaced by a desire-fueled man who had so graciously cooked him breakfast. He certainly needed to be thanked.

Closing his fingers around the base, Milo laved at the tip—first forward, back, and around. Then he brought the head into his mouth and let it graze the inside of his cheek as he did so.

"Ah, fuck!" Kaz pushed his fingers through Milo's hair.

Hollowing his cheeks, Milo sucked, and Kaz grunted through gritted teeth. From the way he kept his ass plastered against the chair, he was trying really hard not to shove into Milo. He glanced up, and the heat in Kaz's eyes fueled him to lick his cock from end to end as he pulled up. Kaz jerked when Milo nipped at one of the veins running along the sensitive underside.

"Jesus," Kaz breathed harshly.

Milo kissed his pulsing member and then rubbed it against his cheek. "But I'm not nearly done with you."

That was when Milo took all of him in until he felt Kaz at the back of his throat, over and over again. Oh, the sounds that came from Kaz then, enough to drive anyone wild. Bobbing his head up and down, making sure to swirl his tongue around him, Milo used his teeth to add to the sensation. Kaz let go of Milo's hair in favor of palming the back of his head while he caressed his cheek and jaw with his other hand.

"That's it," he said, thrusting into Milo's mouth. "Use that delicious tongue of yours."

Encouraged, Milo scraped his fingernails down Kaz's muscular thighs. Kaz gasped in pleasure and bucked his hips in response. Smirking, Milo sucked the entire length of him.

"Fu—uck!"

Kaz's muscles grew taut, and the heat of his release filled Milo's mouth. His throat reflexively swallowed in his hunger. He gave the softening member one last suck and then released it. He sat back on his heels and licked at the corner of his lips, smiling up at Kaz, who was staring at him.

"*Gochiso sama deshita,*" Milo said—the typical response after a meal.

CHAPTER FOURTEEN
BUBBLES

LIKE THE scrumptious breakfast with a side of head, Kaz's bathroom was in the traditional Japanese style, albeit updated to fit the modern architecture of the apartment. The use of it was enough for Milo to forgive him for having to run out. Morning meeting.

He understood those. Thank goodness he didn't have to be at the *Rebel* offices until ten. Cassandra had a morning spa appointment and a visit to her chiropractor, hence the late start.

A typical Japanese bathroom consisted of two spaces. Milo undressed in the entrance room and dropped his borrowed clothes into cloth-lined bamboo baskets. The watery-glass wall tiles and bamboo-wood cabinets were a nice touch.

A little further in was the sink and the actual bathroom, where the shower and a deep bathtub were. The toilet was somewhere else on the premises.

Each area was separated by *shoji* screen doors. It wouldn't surprise Milo if the apartment had a *tatami* tea room to entertain guests in. Kaz seemed like the type to bring the comforts of home with him wherever he went.

Like the rest of the apartment, Kaz's bathroom was extravagant. The tub was custom-made concrete that could be filled to overflowing and had a custom-designed waterfall spout. Steam rose from the water already there. The floor was limestone that incorporated precision laser-cut slots, providing a drain right around the tub so splashing wouldn't be a problem.

In a similar style to the tub was a concrete bench with a shower above it. On a ledge were a shallow wooden bucket, a ladle, and a stool to be used by whoever was taking a bath. Milo imagined sitting behind Kaz on that bench and scrubbing his magnificent back. Then, after they rinsed themselves off, they would step into the tub and....

His cheeks burned. Oh, the things they could do. He had never fucked in a tub before. Not even with.... He pushed away thoughts of Celeste. She no longer had any place in his life. She had moved on, and so should he.

Once naked, he approached the concrete bench and gingerly took a seat, expecting the surface to be cold. Instead, warmth met his skin. Heated floors and bench. An indulgent smile spread across his lips.

He felt spoiled, and he liked it. Liked it a lot.

While he filled the bucket with water for rinsing, he looked out the windows. Behind the bamboo blinds were magnificent views of Central Park. He sighed, imagining late-night soaks. A part of him wondered if he could convert his apartment bathroom into a low-end version of this opulence.

Knowing his building owner might not approve, he upended the bucket of warm water over his head and let go of the idea. Once sufficiently rinsed, he carefully stood up from the concrete bench and made his way to the tub. In a traditional bath, after rinsing, there was an initial soak, which was his favorite part of the process.

The water in the tub was green. That brought another smile to his face. Kaz used green-tea bath salts. The man refused karaoke, but he followed all other traditional Japanese standards. What a contradictory man.

It was what excited Milo about him.

He hissed when he tested the water by dipping in one foot. He had forgotten that the water tended to be relatively hot for this kind of bath. It was meant to relax the muscles and remove all the kinks.

Once his body temp adjusted, he fully submerged himself. He reached for one of the neatly folded face towels, soaked it, wrung out the excess, and placed it on top of his head. Then he scooted lower until even his mouth was underwater. He caught himself thinking this was the life and made a mental note to book a trip to Japan soon.

The second a vacation concretized in his mind, selfish ideas of taking Kaz with him inserted themselves as an addendum to the original plan. Milo could still taste the salt of him in his mouth. Watching the man give himself over to his ministrations that morning was a heady turn-on.

Kaz was usually in complete control. Having him let go because of the pleasure Milo could give came with a sense of power. He wasn't the only one affected in the relationship they had going, which presented a myriad of possibilities. Very pleasing, possibly hot—no, definitely hot—possibilities.

But before all that, they needed to have an uninterrupted dinner to talk things through. He wanted to know what Kaz meant by being "his." Was that his way of saying they were exclusive? Were they even dating?

Sure, they had made each other come, but an orgasm did not a relationship make. If Milo was going to do this, he needed to be aware of the parameters. Were they purely physical? A booty call?

The idea of them having nothing more than sex made his heart ache.

Kaz said Milo made him lose control, that he had to stop himself from encroaching on Milo's daily life, that if it were possible he'd want Milo by his side at all times. As plain as the words were, they still implied many things. He wanted clarity before he could commit to anything.

He hated to think that he was at the point where he would take whatever Kaz was willing to give. It scared him.

This was more than he had with Celeste. This was life-altering stuff. If he got in too deep, it might actually kill him if things went south.

He couldn't have that. He had his career to protect. Most of all, he wouldn't allow his heart to become that vulnerable again. Yet at the back of his mind there lived a sinking suspicion that he was already there.

Annoyed, he slipped the towel from his head and emerged from the tub. He needed to get to work. That meant finishing the bath fast.

He stomped to the bench and reached for the sponge and bottle of liquid soap.

The moment he popped the cap, Kaz's signature scent reached him. Without thinking twice, he brought the bottle to his nose and inhaled. There it was, the spicy musk.

His annoyance melted away at the thought of smelling like Kaz for the rest of the day. It brought a thrill that he didn't expect.

Annoyed again, he squeezed a dollop onto the sponge and began scrubbing himself. He would forego shampooing, because he had his own preferred bath products at home. He just wanted to wash the smell of last night's party off his skin.

A shudder ran through him at the memory of the aphrodisiac. He might never look at a cube of chocolate the same way again.

Only when he rinsed and stepped back into the tub for a final soak did he remember he didn't have any work clothes with him. That cut his bath short. If he wanted to make it to the office before Cassandra, he needed to get home quickly and change.

He stepped out of the tub, toweled off, and contemplated rummaging through Kaz's closet for something to wear that could get him to his apartment in one piece without looking like a boy trying on his father's clothes.

Making up his mind to raid the man's closet anyway, he slipped on one of the robes hanging from a wooden hanger in the entrance room. Then he grabbed a towel to dry his hair and bid farewell to the luxurious bathroom.

"Until next time," he said dreamily as he stepped into the hall.

He was absentmindedly scrubbing excess water out of his hair when he stepped into the living room. At about the same time, Kaz's brute of a driver entered the apartment carrying a garment bag. Milo paused with an embarrassing squeak of surprise.

The driver, who was also Japanese, stopped his forward progress and bowed at the waist. He apologized in Nihongo and introduced himself as Jiro. Milo could only stare at the dragon claw peeking out of the man's collar.

His curiosity brought images of what the entire tattoo could look like. It could be small or massive. And he surely didn't get it in Japan, since there was a stigma attached to having any tattoo. It was usually associated with the *yakuza*.

"McLaren-san?" Jiro straightened. The corner of his lips twitched when he asked in English, "Is everything all right?"

Milo blinked as he recovered from his initial shock at running into someone other than Kaz in his apartment. Of course Kaz had people who could come and go as they pleased.

"Yes. Yes." He shook his head. "I'm pleased to meet you, Jiro-san."

"Please." He raised a large, scarred hand. The tip of his pinky was missing. "Jiro is fine."

"Jiro," he repeated with a smile, attempting to break the awkward tension in the air between them. What must the man think of him and his relationship with Kaz? "If you would excuse me, I need to get ready for work."

Jiro bowed again. "That is what I am here for."

His eyebrow rose unintentionally. What could the large man who was slightly intimidating in an "I can kill you with my thumb" kind of way mean? A shaved head and sunglasses indoors did that.

He indicated the garment bag. "Waka-sama asked me to bring you this. We've taken your measurements off your tuxedo and procured a suit for your use. We've sent the tux to be cleaned and will deliver it to your apartment once it's done. If there's anything unsatisfactory with what I have here, let me know and I can easily find a replacement. If you would like to personally visit a store to acquire a suit to your liking, I have been given instructions to drive you. This also extends to escorting you to work."

In everything that Jiro said, the word that made the biggest impact was "Waka-sama." This was the second time Kaz had been referred to by this term. If his Nihongo was correct, it was one of the old words used to denote the status of someone who was highborn or, at the very least, important.

He wanted to ask about it but was too shy to do so. Would Jiro even tell him? He seemed like the loyal sort. In any case, Milo wanted any information about Kaz to come from the man himself.

"McLaren-san?" Jiro asked again when Milo hadn't responded.

"Please," he finally said, getting his bearings back. "Call me Milo."

Kaz's driver shook his head. "It would be inappropriate for me to be so casual. For the sake of my job security, allow me to continue to be formal with you. Waka-sama would not take kindly to the breach of protocol."

Seeing that the large man's resolve was immovable, Milo reached for the garment bag. He unzipped it and peeled aside the flap to reveal the Hugo Boss suit he'd picked out from the Mercedes-Benz fashion show. With all the commotion, he'd completely forgotten about it.

"How…." His jaw dropped.

"Waka-sama instructed specifically that we procure this suit for you." With an expectant grin, Jiro asked, "Is it to your liking?"

"I… uhm…." He shook his head to clear the shock that muddled his brain. "This is too much. Please let Kaz… ah, Mr. Yukifumi know I can't accept this."

As if on cue, Milo's phone rang. He glanced around for the device and found it sitting on the counter near a bowl of loose change and keys. When he picked it up, his heart skipped.

Kaz's name flashed on the screen, which included a selfie. It was a shot of him from head to collarbone, his hair wet.

But the most captivating of all were his eyes. That piercing stare knifed right through him. God, he was gorgeous. He must have taken it right after his shower the night he brought Milo home drunk. It blew his mind so much that he almost forgot how to pick up.

Before the call could end, he swiped his thumb across the screen and brought the phone to his ear.

"Hello?" he said tentatively.

"Take the suit," came Kaz's command from the other end.

"How?" Again he was reduced to monosyllabic responses.

"Jiro sent me a text when he arrived at the building. I figured you just finished your bath and are currently holding the garment bag. You're not by any chance naked, are you? Because I would hate to have to gouge out my guy's eyes."

"I'm in a robe." He glanced around the living room and squinted at the floor-to-ceiling windows. "Are you spying on me or something? Don't tell me there are security cameras in here and you can actually see me?" Because that would be creepy.

"There are security cameras, but I can't see you. I just knew you wouldn't want to take the suit. Take. The. Suit."

He rolled his eyes. The guy definitely smirked. He could hear it in the amusement in his words, the jerk.

"Kaz, this is too much. I can't."

"On the way to my meeting, all I could think about was you scrubbing your naked body in my bathroom. Then when you were soaking that tight, gorgeous ass in my bath, did you think of me too? Did you touch yourself while thinking of me?"

A flash-fire blush burned across Milo's face. He turned away from Jiro and hurried to Kaz's bedroom.

"Can you not?" he whisper-hissed. "Jiro is in the living room!"

Kaz chuckled.

The sound was dark and lush, like the richest chocolate. It seemed to reach out from within the phone to caress Milo's suddenly overheated skin. It was like being in the tub again, but instead of feeling relaxed, he was all flustered and needy.

"Jiro has many superpowers, but unless you have me on speaker, I doubt he can hear me." He paused. "Were the bamboo curtains drawn while you scrubbed yourself?"

"Of course."

"Good. From now on your body is for my eyes only."

"Kaz…." It was more a moan than the admonition it was meant to be. He was fighting a losing battle.

"Did you imagine what I would do to you in that bathroom? How I would take you in that tub? On that concrete bench? Against the window where someone might see?"

Feeling himself harden at the sensuality of Kaz's tone, Milo exhaled, "Yes."

The growl came loud and clear. "Have dinner with me tonight. This time, we won't be interrupted."

"Dinner?" He bit his lower lip, his hand already pushing between the folds of his robe.

"Yes. Wear that suit, and I promise I will make good on whatever fantasy you have swirling around in that beautiful head of yours."

A delicious shudder ran through Milo's body as he rubbed his cock with slow, sensual strokes. He closed his eyes and said, "With a promise like that, how can I say no?"

"You don't." When Kaz paused again it was as if he knew what Milo was doing to himself. "Because saying yes is so much better."

He moaned.

CHAPTER FIFTEEN
BEWARE

MILO WALKED into the chaos of the *Rebel* offices with an extra bounce in his step. Kasey looked up from her desk as he came in and paused midcall. She put whoever she was speaking to on hold, got up, and rounded her desk to sidle up next to him.

"There's something different about you," she said, assessing him.

"Any messages for me?" He didn't bother asking about messages for Cassandra, because all her correspondence went straight to him. All her calls were rerouted to his phone.

Kasey reached over her desk to retrieve a stack of pink sheets and handed them to him. "You have several confirmations for PFW and phone calls you need to return, especially to the photographer for the autumn jackets shoot."

He rolled his eyes heavenward and prayed for strength. "Did the art director change his mind again?"

"Is that from the Hugo Boss Spring/Summer collection?" Garret squealed. His hair was a jaunty canary yellow. Matched with purple suspenders and pink skinny jeans, he looked like he just walked off a Tim Burton movie set.

Milo endured the scrutiny. They were in fashion, after all. Being looked at was part of the job, especially when he wore a suit that wasn't even on the market yet.

Heat crept up his neck. Kaz. Who knew he was as sexy on the phone as he was in real life?

The man was lethal. Milo was fast becoming addicted, and that wasn't good. It wasn't good at all. Distracting as hell. Still!

He'd never had this many amazing orgasms in his life, and they hadn't even had actual sex yet. Oh, his heart. May it survive the sex god that was Kazuhiko Yuki—

"Oh my God!" Garret interrupted his train of thought with a squeal louder than his previous one. "You got some last night!"

"That's it!" Kasey pointed at Milo, eyes wide behind her ironic hipster eyeglasses that were too big for her face. "You have that just-fucked glow about you."

She and Garret clasped hands and bounced in place as if they had just won a shopping spree inside the infamous *Rebel* closet.

"Finally," Garret gasped, complete with dramatic hand to his chest. "Who is the lucky girl? Or guy?"

"It's about time you got over that bit—"

Milo raised his hand. "As much as I'd like you to talk shit about my ex and bask in the afterglow, you two are wrong. It's the suit."

"No." Garret leaned forward and sniffed him. "I can tell you've had at least one orgasm in the last twenty-four hours. Call it a gift."

Actually, three. But who's counting?

Milo inched away, forcing his hands to stay at his sides to keep from fidgeting with his tie. Could Garret smell Kaz's bodywash on him? He had been sniffing himself like a weirdo during the car ride over, and the spicy musk was definitely evident on his skin.

"Is it the person who keeps sending you flowers?"

Kasey's question pulled Milo back to the comedy show he had walked into. "What flowers?"

Without waiting for the receptionist to respond, he headed straight for his desk. At one corner sat another vase of white calla lilies. They were gorgeous and as elegant as the man who sent them. He snatched the card sticking out of the holder and quickly slipped it out of the envelope.

For this morning and for more like it.

The lovesick teenager returned. He pressed the note to his nose as though the paper possessed any scent other than... paper. Kaz brought out sides of him he didn't know existed. He was caught up in the pace the man set, and it should bother him, but it didn't. What was happening to him?

Cassandra had seen the pictures and read the articles like everyone else. Garret and Kasey wouldn't stop talking about it for days after the news broke. Milo played it off as a publicity stunt, like he'd been told to do, but he had a sinking feeling they would make the connection soon enough. A two-ton weight sat on his chest at the thought of being found out. What was the worst that could happen?

"In my office," Cassandra barked as she passed him. "Now!"

Milo hadn't realized he'd spaced out until his boss walked by in a blur of dove-gray leather. He dropped the card on his desk, picked up his tablet, and hurried in after the fuming editor in chief. After a morning of spa treatments and a visit to the chiropractor, someone must have messed up to put her in a mood. Heads would roll.

"Close the door," she said, shrugging off her floor-length coat and hanging it on the rack at one corner of her office.

Then she proceeded to tug off her gloves. Everything on her body that day was in monochrome, down to the beautiful leather dress with long sleeves and a full skirt that reached her knees. Some might think it was too much, but the whole ensemble was Cassandra to a tee.

He did as he was told and prepared himself for what was to come. Cassandra dropped the gloves on her desk with a *thwack*. Then she pinched the bridge of her nose and breathed with her eyes closed. Her other hand grasped her tiny waist.

"I take it the spa day didn't go well?" he ventured as an attempt to undercut the tension.

Cassandra inhaled sharply, then sent a punishing glare Milo's way. "What's going on with you and Kenji Suzuki?"

"Excuse me?" His grip on his tablet tightened. That came way out of left field.

"Don't play ignorant, Milo." She splayed her hands on her desk and leaned forward. "He's been asking about you."

"He has?" No matter how hard he tried, his brain kept refusing to engage.

"Now you're lying to me."

The accusation snapped him out of his shock. "I'm not lying. Besides a professional relationship, there's nothing going on between me and Suzuki."

"Milo...." Cassandra sighed. She straightened in favor of crossing her arms. "I only forgave you for that debacle at the Hugo Boss show because their entire inventory was sold out in minutes. And it's free publicity for the magazine. But!" She pointed at him. "You know I don't tolerate crazy behavior from my staff. Especially not from you."

He swallowed. It wasn't like he could defend himself. The pictures said it all, no matter how erroneous the allegations in the articles were. Well, except for those who speculated it was a love triangle between him, Kaz, and Tommy. Take his friend out of the equation and they were two-thirds right. But where did Kenji fit into all of it?

"Look, Cassandra," he began, reaching for the truth. "I don't know why Suzuki is asking about me. You know I wouldn't do anything that would put the reputation of this magazine in jeopardy."

The chill in her expression warmed a degree. "Then there's nothing going on with you and Kenji?"

He shook his head, hoping his sincerity showed on his face. "No."

Then he paused. She needed to know. If this thing with Kaz was going anywhere, she needed to know.

"But there might be something with his business partner." There. He said it.

A minute must have ticked by. The silence was palpable between them. Then Cassandra laughed.

Milo's face fell in shock for the second time since he'd entered her office. In fact, she laughed so hard she bent over and hugged herself. He was speechless. A stern warning, he was expecting. Even a command to break things off. Certainly not hysterical laughter.

When Cassandra straightened, she swiped at a stray tear that fell from the corner of one eye. Then she took a deep breath, a wide smile spreading across her face.

"I don't care what you do with Yukifumi," she said. "He's not in our industry, despite being Kenji's silent partner. I spoke about this with your mother. As long as you keep your private life from interfering with your work, I have no problems with it."

Relief came so suddenly that he almost lost his balance. His knees refused to work, and the muscles in his legs turned to jelly.

"Just so we're clear, you're okay with me and Kaz… I mean Mr. Yukifumi…."

"I'm not the one you should worry about," she said in a sudden shift in mood.

The seriousness in her tone told him what she didn't have to say.

With equal gravity, he said, "My father has nothing to do with this."

Her eyebrows arched. "You say that now…."

"Cassandra." This time, it was his turn to pinch the bridge of his nose. "I left that life long ago, and he respects my decision."

"Just be careful." She rounded her desk to stand before him. In her motherly way, she cupped his face and placed a chaste kiss on his lips. "As much as I love you, you know I can't protect you from him."

"No one can." Milo's shoulders slumped.

He reminded himself that he was only living this life because his father allowed it. With the exception of his mother, they were all powerless against the might of Archibald McLaren. In fact, the thought of him ruining Kaz's business if something should go wrong with their relationship chilled Milo to the bone.

Refusing to overthink things, he returned to their previous topic. "Why the sudden panic over Mr. Suzuki?"

Cassandra let go of him, stepped back, and put her editor mask on. "He asked that you meet him for lunch today at Katana."

"That new Japanese restaurant that just opened? I thought it was next to impossible to get a reservation there?"

She waved away his awe. "Apparently he knows the owner. Anyway, he asked for you." The knot between her eyebrows clearly showed she was annoyed by this turn of events, but before Milo could speak, she said, "I said I didn't care about what happens with you and Yukifumi, but remember that these two men are best friends. Kenji's been asking about you. Why? I don't know."

"There's no reason to suspect that what's going on with me and Mr. Yukifumi has anything to do with why Kenji is asking about me." Milo thought back to their first meeting. "He did tease me about being beautiful."

"In any case, you're going to that lunch to find out." Cassandra sifted through the magazines on her desk. "It goes without saying that you need to keep him happy. After his show at Mercedes-Benz and the haute couture show he'll be putting on in Paris, everyone has the House of Suzuki on their radar. We have an exclusive with him. If anything were to jeopardize that…."

What she left unsaid was loud and clear. If Milo messed up, his relationship with Kaz would mean nothing. His job would be on the line.

What could Kenji want with him? It wasn't like they'd spoken more than a handful of times after that first meeting. And never did they speak about anything other than work.

"I'll find out what he wants and see what I can do about it," he said.

"Good." Cassandra pinned him with her I-mean-business stare. "Now, we have much to do before you have to leave. Your reservation is at one. A car will be waiting for you outside the building to take you to Katana."

"Let me print out your schedule for today and grab your messages." He backed out of the office, his relief at Cassandra's acceptance of the possibility of a relationship with Kaz blunted by the mystery of Kenji.

As Milo clicked Print, his phone pinged. A message from Kaz. The smile was instantaneous. The entire world faded away.

He opened the text. *Dinner at 8. Jiro will pick you up.*

And just like that, the buoyancy Milo brought into work with him returned.

Chapter Sixteen
Battlefield

KATANA COMBINED modern Japanese cuisine with a more traditional dining experience. Instead of tables and chairs, the dining space was divided into several *washitsu* with sliding doors, low square tables, and *zabuton* intended for use on tatami mats. Milo had wanted to eat there since it opened. Reservations were tough to get, but he had one for lunch. Regardless of what Kenji wanted to talk about, he was grateful to get a chance to try the top-notch cuisine the foodies were raving about.

A hostess in a black kimono with a red obi greeted him with a bow and the traditional "*irasshaimase*" used to welcome a customer into an establishment. Her hair was in an elaborate *shimada*, which was similar to a chignon, but the strands were gathered together at the crown of the head and a small portion of the bun was sectioned off to point outward.

Admiring the cherry-blossom pin she wore to keep the strands in place, he returned the greeting, gave his name, and mentioned that he was meeting Kenji Suzuki for lunch. She nodded and indicated with a delicate tilt of her head for him to follow.

Servers wearing kimonos in red with black obis carried trays laden with food into several of the washitsu. It seemed Katana's reputation was deserved. Lunch on a weekday and it was as busy as a Friday night.

Milo adjusted his tie. It dawned on him that he was about to sit down with one of the top designers creating a name for himself in the industry. Depending on how the meeting went, it was a milestone in his career.

The contacts he made that day would help in his bid to become the next editor in chief of *Rebel*. The gravity of the situation sunk in as the hostess slid aside the vertical rectangular *fusuma*. He removed his shoes before entering and set them aside.

In the room sat Kenji, wearing an indigo kimono with a deep blue chrysanthemum design embroidered into the rich silk. In such dark fabric, his skin looked paler than usual. His rich burgundy lipstick stood out as he smiled up at Milo.

"Thank you, Akaya," he said to the hostess. "Please ask them to serve."

She nodded and slid the fusuma closed.

"Dozo." Kenji indicated the cushion across from him by stretching his arm out toward it, palm facing the ceiling.

But for Japanese calligraphy on the walls and a bamboo plant in a corner, the room was left bare. The simplicity of the design reminded Milo so much of his days in Japan.

The idea of using his saved vacation days to visit appealed to him more and more as he folded his legs underneath his thighs while resting his buttocks on his heels. The fabric of his pants constricted around him like an anaconda. It had been a while since he sat in the *seiza*-style. He shifted so his ankles were turned outward, silently praying his feet wouldn't fall asleep and his pant seams would hold up during however long the lunch would take, or he wouldn't be able to walk for the rest of the day.

"Thank you for inviting me here, Suzuki-san," he said with a bow. "I've always wanted to try this place."

"My pleasure," he replied with a soft smile and tilt of his head. "Please, call me Kenji. Like Yuki-kun mentioned, we're not in Japan." He reached for the bulbous white narrow-necked ceramic flask on the table. "Sake?"

Milo nodded.

To refuse would be the height of rudeness, even if he didn't like drinking during the day. But since sake wasn't as potent as other forms of alcohol, he could make an exception. This was a business meeting. He needed to follow etiquette or risk offending his host. As a guest, he needed to go with the flow.

Kenji tipped the flask's clear liquid into a small white ceramic cup, making sure he touched his free hand to his pouring arm. He handed the cup to Milo, which he accepted with both hands and a slight bow. Then Kenji raised his own cup.

"Kanpai," he said, tilting his cup.

Milo touched his cup with Kenji's, but he made sure the rim of his was below Kenji's as a sign of respect. The head tilt from his host showed he had done the right thing as they took sips of the warm rice wine.

He savored the acidity—like a mellower version of vinegar. It brought back memories of winter days at an *onsen* in Hokkaido with stunning mountainside views. He ignored the twinge of hurt that accompanied anything that had to do with Celeste.

He promised himself that one day he would be able to look back at that time in his life with fondness. Then images of Kaz and that delectable body of his in a *roten-buro* assailed him, and he remembered his fondness for outdoor hot springs. Milo's cheeks heated almost immediately.

"Too much?" Kenji asked.

"I'm sorry?" he asked back, blinking.

The designer lifted his sake cup. "I chose the more delicate fermentation, considering we're still in the middle of the day. Wouldn't want you stumbling back into the office drunk. Cassandra wouldn't forgive me."

"Oh." Milo admonished himself for letting his imagination get the better of him. He took another sip just to prove his point. "It's actually really good. I was just remembering a time I spent in Hokkaido."

Kenji touched his cheek, a dreamy expression on his feminine features. "Ah, it's been a while since I've taken a bath in an onsen. Their roten-buros are the best."

"Soaking on a cold night with a flask of sake…."

They both shared a sigh of longing.

"Then you must accompany me some time. I know the best place, where the spring is actually located up the mountain."

Kenji moved to refill his cup, but following etiquette, Milo reached for the flask and said, "Let me."

"Thank you." Kenji nodded and nudged his cup toward him.

He poured and spoke. "I would love that. Maybe when we have more time. It's been crazy with the fashion weeks back to back."

Once the cup was full, he picked it up and handed it to his host. The lavender-haired designer thanked him with a slight nod. The delicate dance of their exchange continued.

Milo got the impression that neither of them wanted to make a misstep. Both were circling around something. He was waiting for the real reason why he was invited out for lunch to come to light. What Kenji was waiting for, he could only hazard a guess. And jumping to conclusions would be a fatal mistake, so he prayed for patience.

"Yes." Kenji sighed. "I barely had time to squeeze this meeting with you today into my schedule. My staff and I are busy preparing for Paris."

"I understand." He shifted to alleviate some of the pressure on his legs. The limbs prickled beneath him. "Putting together an haute couture show is no joke. Let me be bold by saying we at *Rebel* are looking forward to that show the most."

His compliment was met with the pursing of lips. "Are you saying you speak for Cassandra as well?"

Milo was taken aback by the question. "Of course. As her assistant, I believe I'm free to express her opinion on the matter of your designs. She's quite taken with your ingenuity, using hemp as your primary fabric. The sustainability alone is astonishing."

Crossing his arms, Kenji cradled his chin in one hand and nibbled on the long fingernail—sharpened to a point—of his pinky. The move emphasized his dark lips even further. Milo swallowed, unsure if he had overstepped.

He replayed their conversation so far.

Cassandra trusted him with her opinions. He'd worked with her long enough to know when she was interested in fostering a certain designer. This year it was Kenji. She raved about his designs and gave countless interviews about them, but before Milo could ask if he had spoken out of turn, the sliding door opened to admit a server balancing a tray in one hand.

The tension in the air dissipated some, and Kenji's seriousness softened when he said, "I hope you don't mind. I took the liberty of ordering for us."

"Not at all," he replied with a cordial smile as the server placed a round plate at the center of the square table.

On its black surface was laid out white paper-thin slices of fish in the sashimi style. The cuts were artfully arranged to resemble a blooming flower with a spiraling petal pattern—like the chrysanthemum embroidery on Kenji's kimono. It was breathtaking.

When the server left, Milo picked up his chopsticks, pulled out one of the slices of fish, and dipped it lightly in a rectangular dish of soy sauce. The second he placed the bite into his mouth and began chewing, Kenji spoke again.

"They say when prepared wrong, *fugu* can be quite poisonous."

The moment Milo's brain processed the meaning of Kenji's words, he stopped chewing and froze, unable to decide if he should swallow or spit out the sashimi.

Fugu was the Japanese word for blowfish. It could be lethally poisonous due to its tetrodotoxin. It needed to be carefully prepared to remove the toxic parts to avoid contaminating the meat.

Not even the most experienced sushi makers in Japan attempted its preparation, because one mistake could mean the death of a consumer. From what Milo had heard, the toxin paralyzed the muscles while the victim stayed fully conscious until he was unable to breathe, eventually dying from asphyxiation. A cold sweat dotted his brow.

As if noticing all the blood leaving Milo's face, a particularly evil smirk crossed Kenji's features. He covered his mouth with the back of his hand and laughed breathily. It was as if the designer intentionally waited until he began eating before mentioning what they were having for lunch. If Milo survived, he vowed to always ask what they were eating before taking a bite.

Unable to take it any longer, he picked up the napkin beside his plate and spit out the masticated fish. He had swallowed some, so if the blowfish was indeed toxic, he already had some of the poison in his system. He glared at Kenji.

Screw etiquette. Trying to poison someone was crossing a really fat line. He picked up his sake and downed the entire cup in an effort to wash away… what? The poison?

It was all going to the same place.

"Why the hell would you do that?" he blurted out after swallowing. He used the back of his hand to wipe at the sake that trickled down the side of his mouth.

The laughter stopped, replaced by the seriousness that Kenji treated him to earlier. "Don't worry. Takashi is the best sushi chef on this side of the world. Fugu happens to be one of his specialties. You will not die today."

Regardless of the relief he felt, he couldn't shake the fact that the man across from him served a potentially lethal delicacy for a reason. His heart wouldn't stop pounding, and his gut screamed at him to leave. But he couldn't do that until he found out the truth, so he called on what little calm he had left to rein in his emotions.

When he was sure his voice wouldn't shake, he asked, "Why did you invite me to lunch, Kenji?"

He intentionally used the designer's first name. Formalities left the building the second he thought he was going to die.

Kenji shifted so he balanced all his weight on his hands as he leaned back on them. He arched an eyebrow and said, "Whatever you have going on with Kazuhiko, I want it to stop."

"Excuse me?" Milo arched his own eyebrow.

A sneer answered his challenge. "You don't know him like I do. He deserves better than some editor's assistant."

Clarity came on swift wings. He didn't know why he was in this situation, because there really wasn't anything between him and Kaz yet. But it seemed someone was marking territory and wasn't afraid to use underhanded tactics to do it.

"And you think you're the one for him?" Milo asked.

"I'm certainly better than you."

"And yet you're here trying to poison me when you should be convincing him."

The statement had Kenji sitting up and scowling. "Kazuhiko has a lot to deal with. The last thing he needs is a distraction."

"Who is to say I'm not the one he's distracting?" Milo asked defensively. The claws were out. "I have a job too. One that I love and have worked hard to cultivate. I didn't ask for Kaz to enter my life, but he did. Forced himself in, even."

"If that's the case, then it shouldn't be difficult for you to end it."

"And why would I do that?"

"Because if you don't, I'm pulling my feature from *Rebel*. There are many other magazines out there that are clamoring for an exclusive."

Milo leaned forward in shock. "That's not possible."

"Of course it is." Kenji rested his arm on the table's lip. "After Paris Fashion Week, I will have solidified my presences in the fashion industry, and I won't need *Rebel*. In fact, *Rebel* will be the one needing me."

He made the mental calculations in his head. Despite what Cassandra said, Kenji's agreement with the magazine hinged upon the results of his haute couture show. If the show wasn't well-received, then Kenji's feature would be downgraded.

But, considering the success of his line during Mercedes-Benz, Paris was a foregone conclusion. For a second, Milo wished the fugu were indeed poisonous. His heart sank when the reality of the threat hit him.

"Consider this your only warning," Kenji added, studying his painted fingernails before pinning Milo with a cutting glare. "Give up on Kazuhiko or I will do more than ruin your career. Am I making myself clear?"

CHAPTER SEVENTEEN
BEATEN

CRYSTAL. THE thought rang loud and clear in Milo's head as he inched away from the table and pushed up to his feet. He bit down on a wince as a serious case of pins and needles assailed his legs. It took years to get used to the *seiza*-style of sitting. He should have just sat cross-legged.

Unfortunately for him, sitting properly was the least of his regrets. He should have known getting involved with someone would lead to drama he wasn't game for.

He broke his promise. He allowed himself to entertain the idea of a relationship again. Hadn't he learned from his experience with Celeste?

There wasn't any room in his heart for love anymore. As far as he was concerned, it was a useless emotion when applied to people. Love was poison. In the case of Kenji, quite literally.

Worst of all?

Because of Kaz, Milo's career was in danger. He wouldn't tolerate threats. Especially not from a designer who was getting too big for his head. He could stand to lose many things except for working at *Rebel*.

The magazine was his life, his future, the only place he felt successful. The alternative was truly frightening. His blood ran cold just thinking about it.

His silence was Kenji's answer.

Turning around, he slid the fusuma aside and stepped out. He should have expected something as underhanded as this. He worked in the fashion industry, after all. He had seen worse, actually participated in a few blackmails under Cassandra's tutelage.

To get what he wanted, he needed to play hardball. Kenji was doing the same thing. Milo had to admire him for that. If he was in love with his best friend, then who was Milo to stand in the way of that?

Kenji could have Kaz if that was what he wanted. Thank goodness they hadn't slept together yet. He could still walk away. Heal. There wasn't much in need of repair to his psyche.

He would lose himself in Paris Fashion Week.

Holding on to the hope of a hectic work schedule to come, he exited Katana into the harsh March weather. With no plans to go back to the office, he pulled his coat tighter around himself and veered left to walk down the sidewalk, away from the town car. He needed to get his head on straight before he returned to his reality.

HE WANDERED the city for what seemed like hours. The sun had begun its descent by the time he arrived at the one place that truly felt like home. His feet hurt as he climbed the steps to the townhouse. Leather shoes were the wrong choice for a long walk, but there was no accounting for everything that happened.

Chilled from the winter that refused to leave, he looked up at the brownstone he spent many of his formative years in. The red door, with its charming owl knocker, never failed to bring a sense of comfort whenever he came home laden with a weary heart.

Considering the time of day, most likely no one was home. It didn't matter, since he needed to be alone. He retrieved the spare key from the left acorn sculpture at his feet and let himself in.

The alarm by the entrance chirped. Closing his eyes in a grimace, he struggled to recall the code. Knowing his mother, it would be something as simple as his birthday, but his father was a whole different bag of tricks. If Archibald McLaren had been home recently, then the security code would be at least ten digits long.

Hoping his mother was the one who frequented the townhouse, Milo opened his eyes and punched in the six digits that represented his birthday. The angry red light turned green, and the chirping stopped. He leaned his forehead against the embossed wallpaper and exhaled a long sigh of relief.

His father was nowhere near the premises. Good. Milo hoped that stroke of luck would continue into the rest of the day.

Milo shrugged off his coat, deposited it into the closet by the front door, and wandered around the elegantly appointed house he once called home—and still did when life got too hard. Stella von Stein had been busy redecorating, he soon discovered.

The once-blue living room was now a sunny yellow with accents of cream and turquoise. The chandelier in the dining room was no longer crystal but ceramic—made in Italy, most likely. And the austere portraits along the hallways and corridors had been switched to soothing garden views.

His lower lip jutted out as he made his way into the modern kitchen. His mother had been quite busy indeed. He wondered if her sudden yen to redecorate extended into his room.

"Milo, *caro mio*," his mother's Italian housekeeper said in her singsong voice when he reached the Sub-Zero. She even pronounced his name as *mee-lo* before tacking on "my dear beloved."

He spun around and flew into the rotund woman's open arms. "Marta! *Mi sei mancato!*" Seeing her cheerful face made him feel a million times better already.

When his mother couldn't take Milo along on shoots because of school, Marta had stepped in as his primary parental figure. She became his surrogate mother and father. She made sure he was fed and dressed, checked his homework, and even disciplined him when he got into trouble.

Ear twisting was her favorite punishment when he forgot to clean his room or pick up after himself. The Italian he knew, no matter how clunky due to the lack of practice, came from her. She crushed him into her large breasts, and then she pushed him back and took his face in both her weathered hands.

"Let me look at you." She gave him a once-over and then gave each of his cheeks a kiss. "My boy, how handsome you are. But too thin. You do not eat enough."

She brought the kind of comfort he needed that day. Maybe that was why he ended up at his mother's townhouse. Knowing Marta would welcome him with the warmth he was used to drew him home like a carrier pigeon. She was his safe place. She had soothed many hurts and healed plenty of wounds.

"What is wrong?" she asked almost immediately when he didn't respond fast enough—like she had some superpower that enabled her to detect when Milo wasn't running at 100 percent.

He deflated in her arms. "Rough day."

"You tell me about it over food."

Like a whirling dervish, she danced around the kitchen. Despite her size, she moved easily, grabbing bowls, spoons, cups, and balancing them in her beefy arms.

Soon ingredients for macaroni and cheese—Milo's favorite comfort food—materialized on the massive counter. But Marta's mac 'n' cheese involved prosciutto, pancetta, four different kinds of Italian cheese, and homemade elbow pasta. Basically, every yummy calorie known to man. His stomach growled in anticipation of the feast.

"It's just work stuff," he said, pulling open the freezer door and scanning its contents.

As much as he wanted to tell her about Kaz and Kenji's ultimatum, he couldn't bring himself to speak about it without breaking down completely. More than a shoulder to lean on, he needed to recharge. Bring himself back to his old self, pre-Kazuhiko Yukifumi.

When he spotted a pint of Ben & Jerry's Karamel Sutra, his heart leaped in appreciation. He grabbed it along with a spoon, though Marta slapped his wrist. Milo gave her a grin and kissed her cheek.

She relented with a stern warning despite the smile stretching her lips. "You will ruin your appetite."

He slid onto a barstool opposite where she worked with scary efficiency and started on the best ice cream flavor in the world—lush vanilla on one side, dark chocolate with chips at the other, and a long column of smooth caramel at the center.

"Then why do you keep it in stock?"

"You know why." She let the smile show fully on her pretty round face.

"Grazie, Mamma," he said, and he meant it.

Warmth suffused his chest as the first sweet bite entered his mouth. It was good to be home.

He switched the topic to something safer—that didn't involve feelings. "Stella's been busy."

Marta frowned at him while she cut the pancetta into bite-size pieces. She saw through his dodge. A part of him was still that fifteen-year-old who couldn't lie to her.

In fact, the truth danced at the tip of his tongue. But another part of him was the grown-ass man who could handle a little heart trouble by himself. Sure, Marta helped significantly during his recovery from Celeste, but that was something major. This with Kaz was a pinprick by comparison.

He huffed when her stare wouldn't relent.

"I'm okay," he said. It was partly the truth. He raised his hand to stall her coming protest when she opened her mouth. "Or I should say I will be okay. I promise, *Mamma*. I know you worry, and I love you for that."

Her face softened. She could never stay annoyed for long when he pulled out the "I love you" card. Like any mother.

She gathered up her fresh elbow pasta, dumped it into the boiling water, and then started on the cheese sauce.

"Signora Stella got it in her head to spend your father's money." She shrugged.

He knew the connotation in her words without her having to elaborate. A prickle began at the back of his neck. "Are they fighting again?"

"You no worry about it, Milo." She waved her hand at him as though she were warding off evil. "Your papa is being a bull. That is all. The signora would have nothing of it."

"Nothing new there." He breathed out the air he held in and took another spoonful of ice cream. The rich caramel at the center fortified him greatly. The longer he spent in Marta's company, the steadier he became.

Then he ventured into dangerous territory by asking, "How is he?"

Marta narrowed her gaze at him, but then concentrated on stirring the cheese, which reminded Milo that he hadn't had anything to eat since leaving the office to meet with Kenji.

"Your papa is fine, but why you ask?"

He sucked thoughtfully on his spoon. "Why not? Just because I'm living my own life outside his control doesn't mean he stops being my father."

She harrumphed. "You live your life. He gave you that gift. You no need concern yourself with him."

The censure in her words was clear. It seemed the women in his life made it their mission to protect him from his father—from Stella to Cassandra to Marta. They all took a stand.

Milo slid off the barstool and rounded the counter until he reached the housekeeper. Then he wrapped his arms around her waist, hugged her tightly from behind, and rested his chin on her shoulder.

"You know I'm only free because he wants me to be, right?"

She said something in rapid-fire Italian about the Devil being a tricky individual who would stop at nothing to get what he wants. Milo wouldn't have understood it all if he weren't standing so close to her. He tightened his hold, knowing her fear. She shared it with Cassandra and Stella. The bravest of men cowered in the presence of Milo's father.

"Thank you for protecting me," he whispered. "Thank you for always being there for me. I cherish that."

She tapped his hands, then said, "Ti amo, ragazzo mio. Now, go wash up. Your food will be ready in ten minutes."

He kissed her plump cheek before letting go. "Can you bring it up to the movie room? I feel like watching something."

Marta nodded and gave him half her focus. His first real smile since lunch blossomed on his face as he returned the ice cream to the freezer and left the kitchen.

With each second that passed, he returned more and more to himself. He pushed away the dark memories involving his father as he jogged up the stairs. There was nowhere else he wanted to be that night.

At exactly ten minutes, he was showered, dressed in his college T-shirt and sweats, and lounging on the plush leather couch of the TV room. *Pacific Rim* was queued up on the hundred-twenty-inch flat screen mounted on the wall. This day called for some *jaeger* versus *kaiju* action. Huge robots fighting undersea aliens never failed to make him feel better.

He pressed Play when Marta came in with a tray. She handed him a huge bowl of the mac 'n' cheese and a vat of her famous virgin sangria. Milo felt so spoiled, he immediately dug in.

"If you want anything else…." She left the rest unsaid as he nodded, smiling, his mouth stuffed full of his favorite comfort food.

He quickly swallowed when she reached the door and said, "I left the suit—"

"I'll have it sent to the cleaners," she said simply.

"*Grazie mille!*"

"*Prego.*"

He was halfway through the pasta when Marta returned to the movie room, phone in hand. She frowned in a way that made him hit Pause and set the bowl aside.

"What is it?" he asked, concern seeping into his words.

She handed him the phone. "For you."

"Thank you." He brought the receiver to his ear. She ran her fingers through his still-damp hair and then left to give him some privacy. "Hello?"

"Milo," Tommy said in an exasperated tone. "The guy who kidnapped you at the Hugo Boss show is here. He keeps switching from English to Japanese and pacing our apartment. I can only understand him half the time." He paused, and Milo's stomach dropped. He knew what his friend was about to say next. "I think he's looking for you. Come home and deal with him, please."

He sighed. Kaz could disappear for days on end, but Milo purposefully missed one dinner and the man went to his home in search of him. He didn't know whether to be touched or scared. Was it too much to ask for a day to himself to figure shit out?

The moment Tommy hung up he knew there wasn't any point in avoiding the inevitable. The longer he stayed away, the harder it would be for the both of them. Kenji didn't give him a hard deadline, but Milo figured he meant him to end things before Paris Fashion Week. The muscles in his chest constricted.

Chapter Eighteen
Broken

ON THE cab ride over, Milo rehearsed his breakup speech. He had it all planned out. He would walk into the apartment with all the confidence he possessed and ask Tommy to give them some privacy. Then he would lay it all out.

His career came first, and their relationship was causing him to lose focus. Of course, there wouldn't be any mention of Kenji and the threats the designer made. The last thing he wanted was to cause friction, not only between friends, but between business partners, which would ultimately blow back on Cassandra and the magazine.

Good thing they hadn't gone too far. Good thing they hadn't spent that much time together. Or that they hadn't gotten to know each other better.

Cutting things off was for the best. They could still move on with their lives as though nothing had happened between them.

The instant the thought settled in his mind, his heart clenched. The pain was so unexpected that he bent over and clutched his chest, and the cab driver asked if he was all right. Unable to speak, he raised his hand and waved away the concern. Then he took a deep breath and sat back against the seat.

Beneath his palm, his heart beat erratically. It was enough to steal his breath. His rib cage seemed to shrink with each inhalation. No matter how hard he tried, he couldn't get enough oxygen into his body, leaving him light-headed.

Despite feeling like he was about to die, he knew what he needed to do. They couldn't continue, for both their sakes.

Ready or not, once the cab pulled up to the curb of his building, Milo stepped out and faced his fate.

The doorman greeted him a good evening. Normally, he would respond, but that night all he could muster was a tight grin. Looking straight ahead, he made a beeline for the bank of elevators.

Thankfully one opened to release a tenant who came down to walk her dog. Her greeting went unacknowledged as he pressed the button to his floor and fished out his keys from the pocket of his sweatpants.

He hadn't bothered changing into something more formal, like a suit. It was a waste of time. Get it over with. That was the phrase that kept repeating itself in his mind as he stuck the key into the lock. Right as he pushed inside, a raised voice assaulted his ears.

"Why won't you tell me where he is, bakayarou?"

Kaz's frustrated question, said in that commanding tone of his, was enough to make Milo pause at the entrance. The man still looked impeccable in the three-piece suit he'd walked out of the apartment in that morning.

Was it just that morning that he'd cooked Milo breakfast with such care?

So many hours ago. A perfect time, where the outside world didn't exist. Why couldn't they rewind and stay in that moment of bliss forever?

Yet there was no ignoring Kaz.

He seemed so big, pacing in the common area of the two-bedroom Milo shared with Tommy. No matter how hard Milo tried, he couldn't help but stare in admiration at the fuming Japanese businessman. Strands of his straight, black hair fell over his forehead from shoving his fingers into them again and again.

Milo ached to touch him and brush those strands away, but it wasn't that simple. Not anymore.

"Finally!" Tommy exclaimed from the couch, raising both hands and then dropping them. "What took you so long?"

No matter how many times he rehearsed the scenario, Milo wasn't prepared for the power of those blue eyes on him. Kaz had a way of looking at him that seemed to unearth all his secrets—like the man knew him to the furthest reaches of his soul. Longing, worry, then dread flitted through Kaz's features.

Milo must not have been hiding his grief well enough. He dropped his gaze to the hardwood floor and gave in to combing his fingers through his still-damp hair.

"Tommy, will you give us a minute alone, please?" Milo didn't know how he managed to speak without his voice trembling.

"You sure?"

He lifted his gaze to look past Kaz's shoulder at his friend, who stood. "Yeah."

One thing he liked about Tommy? He listened.

He might fight Milo on his decisions from time to time, but when asked to do something, he never hesitated. He rounded the suddenly still Kaz and squeezed Milo on the shoulder. Then he grabbed his coat and left the apartment.

No matter how gently Tommy pulled the door closed, the click still caused Milo to jerk in surprise. They were finally alone, and the silence was heavy. Kaz stared intently at him, and Milo opened his mouth to begin his carefully crafted speech, but words failed him at the last second. It also didn't help that his throat refused to relax.

"Where were you?"

The question made him meet Kaz's gaze. It was asked so gently that the worry laced with the words broke Milo's heart. How he wanted to cross the distance between them and just sink into those powerful arms he knew deep down wouldn't deny him access.

Maybe not after that night. Not after what he was about to do for the sake of his career.

"Jiro came to pick you up, but you weren't at work. He told me the woman at the front desk said you left for lunch and never came back. No one would tell me where you were. Not even that jerk you call a friend."

Milo silently thanked Tommy for his loyalty. He might not know the circumstances, but he knew to call the townhouse first. Sometimes he counted it a miracle to have someone like him in his life.

"I needed some time to think," Milo was finally able to say around the cottony texture the inside of his mouth became.

"I was worried about you."

"I'm a grown man and can certainly take care of myself." Milo let the spark of annoyance grow. If that was what would help him get through the night, then so be it. "Last I checked, I don't need to tell anyone where I am, let alone you."

"I don't understand." Kaz took a step forward. "What happened between my texting you about dinner plans and now?"

As if an invisible force pushed him, Milo moved toward the kitchen. Maybe something for his dry mouth would help. Feeling Kaz's intense gaze on his back, he opened the fridge door, pulled out a bottled water, twisted the cap, and took a long swig.

His throat worked too hard. If he swallowed wrong, he'd choke. Kaz waited for him to finish. When only half the bottle remained, Milo closed his eyes and inhaled deeply. On the exhale, he stabbed the man standing across the room from him with the cold stare he reserved to scare the interns.

"This is not working," Milo said, managing finality in his tone.

"What isn't?" Kaz asked back, confusion replacing his worry.

He pointed the bottle at himself, then at Kaz. "This. You and me. I should have known better than to start something with you."

"Nande?"

The question came out in a hoarse whisper. If Milo thought his heart had already broken earlier, it broke even more the moment Kaz's shoulders fell. He was an innocent bystander in all of this. Now he was about to become collateral damage.

Milo had to concentrate, somehow pull back to his brain the blood that had migrated to the soles of his feet.

"My work comes first," Milo said, barely maintaining what little control he had left. "Ever since I met you, my performance has slipped. You're Japanese, you should understand what it means to excel at a job."

"I don't buy it," Kaz growled. "You're lying."

"Think what you want. It won't change the fact that I'm backing away from whatever the hell this is we've got going on. With Paris Fashion Week coming up, I can't afford to drop the ball if I want to make editor by the end of the year."

Kaz took another step forward, fists balled at his sides. "You're lying."

"I'm telling you the truth," Milo grit out. The plastic of the bottle crunched as his hand closed around it.

"I don't think you are."

The hope mixed with pain in Kaz's words ultimately became Milo's undoing. Knees shaking, he put the half-crushed bottle on the counter and leaned his hands over the edge to hide the fact that he could barely stay upright.

"It doesn't matter," Milo said when he regained some of his composure.

"Tell me the truth and I'll fix it," Kaz said. "You have to let me fix it."

Milo's grip tightened on the counter as he forced himself to say between clenched teeth, "I *am* telling you the truth."

Had the designer known that Kaz wouldn't take no for an answer? Wouldn't believe his reason for breaking up? Or maybe Milo wasn't convincing enough.

An almost Zen-like calm came over Milo, allowing him to push off the counter and cross his arms over his chest. He lifted his chin. Kaz needed to believe that he was telling the truth.

Saying it was over wouldn't be enough. He needed to believe that there was no room for him in Milo's life.

"I never thought of you as someone desperate," he said, the words tasting foul in his mouth. "Stop this pathetic attempt of yours to keep us together. I've made up my mind."

Kaz shook his head. "You don't know what you're saying."

But the heat of hurt in Kaz's eyes was unmistakable. He hit a nerve by going after Kaz in that way. Milo was playing dirty and Kaz didn't like it. Not one bit.

With new resolve granting him much-needed strength, he looked Kaz in the eyes as he said through clenched teeth, "I will *always* choose my career over you."

The serious mask Kaz wore broke, revealing a bewilderment that should have sent triumph coursing through Milo's veins. Instead, he hated himself to his core. He had accomplished the impossible and blackened his soul in the process.

In stunned silence, Kaz stepped back, widening the chasm that Milo dug between them. Then carefully, almost reverently, he picked up the trench coat he had draped over the back of the couch. With measured movements, he shrugged it on and pulled up the collar.

Biting down to keep from saying anything else, Milo watched Kaz stride toward the door of his apartment—his head down, his shoulders slumped forward, the pride he once wore no longer evident in his demeanor.

The closing of the front door seemed to echo in the empty apartment. A sense of great loneliness came over Milo. It was the price he had to pay.

Incredibly heartsick, he leaned against the fridge and slid down to the floor, where he curled into the smallest ball he could manage and wept.

Chapter Nineteen
Bearings

CLOSE TO one in the morning, Milo stumbled into his Paris hotel room exhausted and running on fumes. Fashion Week swept him up in a whirlwind of shows, parties, press conferences, luncheons— anything that had to do with clothes—and the week was only half over. He still had a whole host of events to attend with Cassandra and the *Rebel* team, including a gala the magazine was hosting.

That year his heart wasn't in it. What used to be fun just seemed routine. His movements were mechanical.

He accomplished all his tasks efficiently, for sure, and Cassandra had no complaints. Yet each day seemed like an out-of-body experience. As though he watched himself working instead of actually being 100 percent present. Hollow was his middle name.

He toed off his shoes, shrugged off his jacket, and left both articles of clothing on the floor as he stumbled his way onto the bed. He didn't even waste energy with tie removal as he landed facedown on the sheets and pillow.

The dark oblivion of sleep claimed him as he turned over onto his back, but the dream came soon after.

Large hands ease him onto his back. He goes willingly, sighing with relief at being arranged into a more comfortable position. Long fingers comb through his hair and massage his scalp. He moans in appreciation, which is cut short by the press of lips against his.

A series of soft kisses coaxes his mouth open. A tongue darts between his teeth, inviting his into a dance as old as kissing itself.

The bittersweet taste of bourbon jolted him out of the dream like a flash of lightning. Kaz tasted of burnt apple and Marlboros.

Scotch and cigarettes. And come to think of it, the smell was different too. Instead of the spicy musk that never failed to turn him inside out, a cooler scent entered his lungs from cologne he was all too familiar with.

His eyes sprang open as he splayed his hands on a lean chest and pushed, effectively breaking the contact between lips. The light he'd left on at the entryway illuminated the intruder—lush brown hair, day-old scruff, and bright green eyes.

"Tommy?"

In response, Tommy closed his fingers around Milo's wrists and secured his hands above his head. The position brought back memories of the night that broke his world. Panic rose with the relentless drumbeat of his heart.

His breathing hitched. He struggled for air, but before he could protest, Tommy's mouth was on his again. The kiss was punishing. Milo wouldn't be surprised if his lips were bruised in the morning.

As a way of defending himself, Milo did the only thing he could think of before his mind shattered—he bit down on Tommy's lower lip, hard enough to cause pain but not hard enough to actually puncture the skin. As expected, his would-be molester backed off with a startled yell. He positively reeked like an unclean bar.

Milo used the momentum of Tommy's fall to sit up and regain his bearings, He grabbed Tommy by the collar, hauled him to the bathroom, and shoved him into the shower closet. With a twist of the knob, icy droplets rained down on Tommy, eliciting a yelp that was soon followed by shivering and harsh breathing.

When the drunk tried to get away from the spray, Milo kicked him back down and said, "You're not going anywhere, Mister."

"What the hell?" Tommy blubbered out, hair plastered to his head, suit ruined, lips trembling.

"Shouldn't I be the one asking you that?"

Tommy pushed away the strands that covered his face and looked up at him. "I love you."

The three words came at Milo like a physical blow. If he wasn't holding on to the glass door of the shower, he would have stumbled back.

"Excuse me?"

"What don't you get? I said I love you."

"You're drunk."

"I'm sober enough to know I'm telling the truth."

"This can't be happening." Milo rubbed a hand down his tired face. "Please tell me this can't be happening."

"Why the hell not?" Tommy pushed to his feet, but he made no move to step away from the spray.

The warning glare Milo sent him was enough to keep him in place. "Because I don't have the emotional strength for this bullshit right now."

"It's not bullshit. I'm just telling you the truth."

"Then why now?"

Milo questioned his sanity in that moment. Had he stepped into an alternate dimension? Or he was dreaming. Yeah.

It had to be some sort of sick dream. He pinched his arm. A red welt rose over pale flesh.

"What are you doing?" Tommy asked, concern marring his handsome features.

"It hurts," he said dumbly.

"I would imagine so."

"Then I'm awake."

Tommy bowed his head and chuckled. "I don't know whether to be hurt or insulted."

"I'm the one who should be insulted."

"Ouch! Low blow."

"Not low enough." Milo eyed his friend's groin, sorely tempted to aim a well-placed knee in its vicinity. "What the hell do you think you're doing coming to my room drunk, taking advantage of me while I slept, and now confessing that you love me? Did you hit your head on the bar you were at before you stumbled your way in here? And how the hell did you get in anyway? I know I locked the door."

"Spare key."

Two simple words. Of course.

He always gave his spare key to Tommy and vice versa in case one of them lost their key or forgot to bring it. Milo had never regretted that practice until that night. He massaged his forehead. An aching throb began behind his left eye.

"Answer me this," he said, meeting the sincerity in Tommy's gaze head-on. "What's gotten into you?"

"Will you at least let me step out of the shower first?" Tommy asked back. "I think my lips are turning blue."

His lips were indeed turning pale.

Taking pity on the wretch, Milo stepped aside and threw a towel at him, which he caught without missing a beat. Then he backed away until he reached the doorway, needing the safety that space provided. He crossed his arms as a precaution against the urge to throw a punch. He would reserve those for later, depending on the answer to his question.

Tommy draped the towel over his head and began removing his clothes.

"What the hell do you think you're doing?" Milo blurted out, an unexpected blush creeping across his face. He had seen Tommy naked before. Why should this instance be any different?

Tommy gestured to his sodden suit. "If I want to dry myself, I need to remove my clothes. I still have to walk the YSL show tomorrow. Wouldn't want to be sick while doing it."

He had Milo there. As ludicrous as the situation had been so far, he didn't want to be the one to blame if one of the top models in the business called in sick.

Taking a bracing deep breath, he said, "Fine."

Tommy made quick work of peeling off every article of clothing until he was down to his boxer briefs.

"Those stay on or I'm calling hotel security and kicking you out of here," Milo said when Tommy hooked his thumbs into the waistband.

"Harsh." But he reached for one of the bathrobes and put it on. Only then did he start drying his hair. "You're a total mess."

Milo's eyebrow arched up. "What's that got to do with you suddenly feeling the urge to confess?"

"Let's face it, I've been in love with you since that bitch Celeste left."

"I'm having a hard time believing you. Maybe this is my mind playing tricks on me. I think I've been working way too hard."

Tommy gave him a drawl stare, hair still dripping. "Then there's that bastard Japanese guy. And don't deny that there's something going on there, because you were an absolute zombie the next morning. You're forgetting I know that look very well."

"So, you think because I'm a mess that it's the right time to tell me how you feel?"

A long pause followed.

Tommy brought the corner of the towel to his lips, and Milo's brow crumpled. Why did he have to look so damn good in that moment? Staying mad at him would have been so much easier if he were less attractive and not his friend.

"I'm sick and tired of putting you back together after someone goes in and breaks your heart," Tommy finally said.

"Then you end the friendship. Don't decide to say 'I love you'!"

The glare he got for his exclamation stabbed right through him. "Do you honestly think I'd walk away now?"

"Tommy...." Milo returned to rubbing his forehead. The lack of sleep was getting to him. He was seeing double. "You're not making any sense. Let's say I even believe what you're saying. You're the biggest slut I know. What makes you think a monogamous relationship would work? Or do you think I'm the type who would tolerate cheating?"

Another chunk of silence followed, this one brief.

"And don't even think of justifying sleeping around," he headed Tommy off.

"I'm not," came the unexpected reply.

That night was getting more and more insane by the minute. Milo didn't know what to believe anymore. And he thought his relationship with Kaz was complicated.

"Then you need to clarify, because I'm not a mind reader."

Tommy looked him in the eye when he spoke. "I'm saying I'm willing to try if you let me."

"Let you what?" he was almost too afraid to ask.

"Let me love you."

There was that word again. It seemed to steal all the air in the room.

"Tommy." He sagged against the doorframe. His legs barely kept him upright. "I honestly can't deal with this right now."

"Is it because you have feelings for that Japanese guy?"

"Kaz. His name is Kaz."

"I don't need to know his name."

When Milo sighed, his shoulders slumped forward. Then he shook his head. "What can I say to make you understand?"

In a rush of movement, Tommy was on him, grabbing his arms and towering over him. "Tell me you don't have feelings for him."

The last of his strength fled. "You know I can't do that."

"Why not? It's simple. I'm here. He's not."

"Until when will you be here?" Milo challenged. "You're as busy if not busier than I am. How do you think a relationship between us would work?"

"Are you saying you're willing to try?"

Milo shrugged out of Tommy's hold. "Don't twist my words around!"

"Then you have to at least let me try. I know I can be a better boyfriend than that—"

"If you call him 'Japanese guy' one more time—"

"You'll what?" Tommy interrupted his interruption.

"God!" He rubbed both hands over his face. "I'm too tired for this. I have to get up in a couple of hours."

"This would all be simple if you just gave in."

"Give in to what?" Milo fell back onto the couch and leaned forward until his elbows touched his knees. He cradled his heavy head in his hands.

"Let me love you."

"Don't you touch me," he hissed as Tommy laid a hand on his shoulder.

"You know what…." The gorgeous model raised both his hands in surrender. "Maybe this was all a big mistake."

"You're kidding, right?"

"Actually, I've never been more serious in my life." He threw the towel over the back of the couch and walked toward the door. Then he stopped. "You know. All those people I fucked? They were just warm bodies to share my cold bed. Every time I was in someone—man or woman—I imagined you. All I ever wanted was you."

Long after Tommy left, Milo stared at the space he once occupied and tried to make sense of the bizarre conversation. So much for getting any more sleep.

CHAPTER TWENTY
BARGAIN

IT SEEMED the entire city celebrated the success of the House of Suzuki couture show. It certainly looked that way during the *Rebel Gala*, where conversation buzzed about how structural yet strangely wearable the gowns were. Words like *innovative, genius,* and *the future of fashion* were bandied about.

Already the women were swooning over which ones to purchase. There wasn't any doubt about Kenji's talent. Cassandra sure knew how to pick them.

The expert use of fabric to create almost impossible angular shapes brought Milo to tears. Each garment resembled a moving sculpture. He couldn't deny the beauty in the artistry of Kenji's work.

Yes, he mourned the loss of what could have been with Kaz, but after watching what might have been the most magnificent show in Paris Fashion Week history, he knew he had done the right thing. It would have been a great shame for the magazine to lose its exclusive with House of Suzuki because of his feelings for the designer's best friend and business partner.

All was right with the world.

Except... as he stood in the middle of the opulent ballroom, Milo never felt more alone in his life. He lifted a champagne flute from a passing waiter who was dressed like a samurai and downed its contents in several swallows. The bubbles went straight to his head, and he swayed for a moment, but he regained his footing, deposited the empty glass on another passing tray, and liberated a fresh one.

Getting drunk as fast as he could seemed like a great plan. Cassandra gave him the night off as a reward for good work. He could have done better if he weren't a zombie half the time from lack of sleep. Damn dreams. But waking up with the memory of Kaz in his mouth mattered little at that point.

In the morning the team would fly back to New York, and everything would be business as usual.

Except... how could it be business as usual when he felt nothing inside?

And he hadn't seen his wayward friend since the night Tommy confessed his misguided feelings. It might be a good idea to spend some time apart.

Milo still couldn't fathom what drove Tommy. It certainly wasn't sex. Copious amounts of liquor, yes, but in all their years as friends, he'd never thought of Tommy as someone who fell in love. Until recently, he wasn't even sure the guy had a heart to give away.

Feeling a little light-headed after his second glass, Milo wound his way through the crowd. Hundreds of red-paper lanterns hung from the ceiling, giving the space a moody atmosphere. Potted miniature cherry-blossom trees were scattered along the walls and strung with white twinkle lights.

Instead of hors d'oeuvres, he was presented with a live sushi bar with chefs flown in from the Land of the Rising Sun, which seemed to go over well with the assemblage. They were supposed to create an East Asian atmosphere, but Milo knew there was nothing authentic about the party.

Normally, the fake wouldn't bother him. He worked in an industry that thrived on it, after all. But with everything that had happened, stomaching the superficial gave him gas. At least his feelings for Kaz had been real—intense to the point of earth-shattering, but real.

He must be a masochist to continually put himself through that torture. A chuckle escaped him. It was over. He ended things. He needed to live with the consequences.

As if the mere thought of Kaz conjured him up, the crowd parted to reveal the stunning Japanese businessman in a tux. Hurt warred with desire in Milo's chest.

All that gorgeous black hair was slicked back. It begged for fingers to rake through it while in the middle of a passionate embrace.

Milo's mouth watered as a myriad of lurid thoughts assailed him at the sight of Kaz. He would never admit it aloud, but he actually missed Kaz. Even impassive, his face was still strikingly handsome. He had one hand in his pocket, while the other rested on—

"Not even a month since you two broke up, and already he has his hand just shy of a supermodel's ass." Tommy materialized as if from thin air. "I'd say it's looking like you don't mean anything to him."

As much as he wanted to hate Tommy in that moment, his words took root. Milo couldn't unsee what was happening before him. And as much as he wanted to pretend Kaz wasn't practically fondling the reed-slim slip of a girl who looked barely legal, the evidence was so in his face that he couldn't look away. Milo felt like he was a car wreck and everyone slowed down to stare at him.

"Did you really mean what you said the other night?" he found himself saying without really thinking of the consequences of his words.

"Are you going to use me to make him jealous?" his friend asked back.

Milo looked up at him. Maybe a relationship between them could work. He'd never entertained the idea before. Why not?

"And what if that's the plan?" No harm in going with the truth.

Tommy's eyes narrowed. "On one condition."

"What is it?"

"You need to tell me why you broke up with him in the first place."

The benevolence in his tone took Milo aback. "I don't understand."

"It's obvious you're in love with him for you to stoop so low as using my feelings for you to make him jealous." Tommy wrapped his arm around Milo's shoulders and pulled him in close. The rest of his words he whispered into Milo's ear seductively, sending shivers down his spine. "So you need to give me context if I'm going out on a limb for you."

The blush didn't come from their close proximity to each other. Milo was mortified with himself. He thought he had been right ending things with Kaz. He thought he prioritized his career more. But seeing him with someone else? After Kaz had boldly claimed ownership of him?

"I'm a horrible person." He dropped his gaze. "I shouldn't manipulate you like this."

"It's not manipulation if I'm aware of what's happening." Tommy placed a kiss on his temple. "So, what happened?"

"But the other night—"

"Forget about it. I was drunk. After some much-needed reflection, I knew you were right. I was taking advantage of the situation without thinking things through."

Milo tilted his chin up so he could look into those startling eyes the color of moss. "How did I get so lucky to have someone like you in my life?"

"All right." Tommy grinned a charming smile. "My ego is sufficiently inflated. Are you going to tell me or what?"

Milo placed a hand on his friend's chest and sighed, inching closer so the only barriers between them were the clothes they had on. "Kenji threatened to pull his exclusive from *Rebel* if I didn't break things off."

Tommy pulled him even closer, if that were possible—they were practically hugging—and muttered into Milo's hair, "That son of a bitch."

The shrug came and went. "I can't blame him. He's in love with Kaz."

"What's that guy got that I don't?"

"An extra-large dick."

At the joke, Tommy threw his head back and laughed, drawing the attention of everyone within hearing distance. Ashamed at the attention they were getting, Milo hid his face in the crook of his friend's arm. Then Tommy's lips were on his ear again.

"You're doing good," he whispered. "He's looking this way."

"He is?"

But before Milo could turn to check, Tommy shifted so all he could see was the model's shoulder. "Don't look. He'll know we're bluffing. Just keep doing what you're doing and flirt like your life depends on it."

He plastered a rueful smile on his face as he looked Tommy in the eye again. If he focused on his face, Milo wouldn't have to hear the extreme pounding of his heart.

"And remember," Tommy said with a saccharine smile, "no one can force you to do anything you don't want to. So what if Kenji is in love with Kaz? You're the one he wants."

"But my career…."

"Nothing will happen to it just because one designer decides to go postal. In our world, you're in one day, then the next you're out."

"Are you seriously quoting a reality TV show at me right now?"

"But it's the truth."

Of course it was the truth. Fashion ate new designers for breakfast and shit out old ones. It was a dog-eat-dog world, and those who weren't fast enough died in a gutter with the fashion victims and has-been trendsetters.

"If you really love him, then nothing should stop you from having him." Tommy placed a kiss on his forehead before he bent down in search of Milo's mouth.

Milo closed his eyes to accept the kiss, even if he thought it was going a little too far. Everything was going to be okay. At least he hoped it would.

The lips he expected never landed. Instead, he was yanked away from Tommy's hold so abruptly that when he opened his eyes, a wave of dizziness assailed him. He took several deep breaths to keep down the bile threatening to climb up his throat before he could get a sense of what was happening.

The giant wall of Kaz's back blocked his view of Tommy. Somehow, the guy had pulled him out of his friend's grasp and positioned him behind his bulk..

"What the hell do you think you're doing?" Milo asked indignantly.

Without taking his feral gaze away from Tommy, Kaz said, "He was about to kiss you."

"We're not doing this here." Milo looked around at the mix of concerned and curious faces surrounding them. He tugged at the arm he clung to. "Come on, Kaz. Come with me."

"I think you should—"

"Shut up, Tommy," Milo hissed.

The last thing he needed was a brawl. Cassandra wouldn't forgive him, and by now Kenji would have caught wind of what was happening. He was all for making Kaz jealous, but not to the point of causing any more of a commotion. They needed to get out of there.

"Are you sure about this?" Tommy pressed.

Milo positioned himself between the still-fuming Kaz and Tommy inches away from the grave. "Thank you. I'll take it from here."

He lifted his hands in surrender and backed away. "Then my job is done."

"What does he mean?" Kaz growled as Tommy disappeared into the crowd.

Turning around to face the man he could no longer deny he had feelings for, Milo said, "Take me to your hotel room."

In an instant, all the anger drained away from those cool blue eyes, replaced by a heat Milo had missed fiercely.

"Are you sure about this?" Kaz asked in Nihongo.

Sending a silent prayer of gratitude for the dispersal of the gathered onlookers, he nodded. "I've never been surer about anything in my life."

Taking his hand, Kaz led them to the exit. A thrill went through Milo as he eagerly followed. Kaz hadn't even bothered taking his leave.

146

Kenji would surely be fuming before the night was out, but the sense of satisfaction he felt at the thought of pissing off the designer who threatened to poison him made the possible fallout worth it. He would apologize to Cassandra in the morning.

CHAPTER TWENTY-ONE
BARE

THE INSTANT Kaz opened the door to the presidential suite at one of the most expensive hotels in Paris, Milo whirled around and brought their lips together in a hungry, fevered kiss. A mad dash of emotions had ridden him since they left the gala. He needed Kaz—physically, emotionally, in every way he could get him.

Without waiting for entry, he pushed his tongue into Kaz's mouth, luring his tongue out to play. Kaz grunted, whether from how forceful Milo was being or from pleasure, Milo wasn't sure. He looped his arms around Kaz's neck and kept him from going anywhere while Kaz circled his waist with those powerful hands.

When Kaz pulled his tongue back, Milo wrapped his lips around the tip and sucked, giving Kaz a preview of what he intended for that night. The answering growl told Milo he did the right thing. It excited him further.

His body felt so hot he was sure he would melt if they continued down that frantic road. In an effort to slow things down, he moved his lips to Kaz's cheek, up to his ear, and then down to the strong column of his neck.

Breathing hard, Kaz lifted Milo up and marched the rest of the way into the suite. Milo held on as he was carried into the bedroom and dropped onto the bed. Kaz resumed the kiss, but at a languorous pace. He savored the exploration of the inside of Milo's mouth, and Milo loved that Kaz tasted of the burnt apple he came to expect from the scotch Kaz favored. He'd missed the bitter sweetness of it.

Like Milo had done earlier, Kaz kissed a trail from the corner of Milo's lips to his jaw. Milo lifted his chin to give Kaz better access to his neck and wherever else he wanted to go from there. But the kisses never came. Instead the warmth of the large body over his disappeared.

Milo's moan of pleasure turned into one of confusion as he opened his eyes to see Kaz standing at the side of the bed. Those cool eyes searched Milo, and then Kaz's lips turned into a rigid line, giving his handsome face an edge.

"What's going on here?" Kaz finally asked after a long beat of silence.

Pushing himself up to his elbows, Milo sighed. "If I have to tell you, then I'm not doing it right."

"Why are we here?"

"Maybe because I want you. And you clearly want me." Milo sat up the rest of the way and hooked his fingers into the waistband of Kaz's pants. Then he cupped the bulge straining the fabric, begging to be freed from its constriction.

With a hiss, Kaz stepped away from the touch. "You said we were over. You said that your career will always take precedence. What changed?"

Confusion turned into annoyance. "For someone who claims to own me, you certainly have a funny way of showing it."

Kaz's blue eyes narrowed dangerously. "What game are you playing?"

"You were practically molesting that girl at the gala." Milo pushed to his feet and got into Kaz's face. He had to look up because of their height difference. "Don't think I didn't see your hand on her ass."

"And what about you and Tommy?" Kaz challenged, switching to Nihongo. "Are you two dating now? Or just fucking?"

"How dare you bring Tommy into this," Milo said between clenched teeth.

Several red flags rose in Milo's mind, but he ignored every one of them. Let Kaz be angry. Let the both of them fight it out. Because it was clear that no one was getting fucked that night.

Kaz grabbed his arms and shook him. "You brought Tommy into this. Don't think I don't know that you were intentionally baiting me. What I don't understand is why?"

The last part was said in English in a calm, calculating voice. It scared Milo more than Kaz's previous anger. An irate bull of a man, Milo knew how to handle. But someone calm was truly dangerous.

"I think this is a mistake," Milo said, dropping his gaze. He stepped away from Kaz's grasp and ran his fingers through his already mussed hair. "This is all a mistake. I have to go."

Kaz closed his long fingers around Milo's arm and flung him across the bed. Then, with deliberate movements, he removed his jacket, loosened his bow tie, and flung both articles of clothing to the floor.

"What are you doing?" Milo asked, breathless.

"I'm giving you what you want," Kaz said, deliberately removing his platinum cufflinks one at a time and placing them on the bedside table.

Milo tried to stand, but as soon as he gained purchase, Kaz pushed him back onto the mattress. Then he returned to undressing. He eased each button with maddening slowness, baring that delectable skin of his one inch at a time.

"Kaz, please." Milo's mouth watered.

His throat refused to work properly the instant his eyes landed on the bumps of muscle that made up Kaz's abs. He was ripped, even more than the last time he had seen Kaz bare-chested. But he studied the man for an entirely different reason. He reached out and closed his hand around Kaz's hip.

"You've lost weight," Milo murmured.

Kaz removed the cummerbund of his tux and threw it aside as he'd done with the jacket and tie. "What does it matter to you? I would think there's only one part of me that you need at the moment."

The words hurt. They really did. But Milo had no idea why.

He lifted his gaze to meet Kaz's and noticed the dark circles beneath his eyes. Without putting much thought into his actions, he lifted his hand from Kaz's hip to trace the deep lines bracketing those stern lips.

"I did this," Milo whispered, surprised the words made it past the lump in his throat.

Kaz leaned into the touch, cupped Milo's hand against his cheek, and placed a kiss at the center of his palm. Milo felt that kiss all the way to his gut. It clenched in pain as though he'd been sucker-punched.

"What happened that night?" Kaz asked against Milo's palm, his breath hot against Milo's skin. "Why did you change your mind?"

"Why were you with that model?"

Those blue eyes turned to ice. "Because I didn't want to be alone knowing I would be in a room with you in it."

All of Milo's defenses crumbled with that one admission. "Kenji is in love with you."

"What?" Kaz searched Milo's face as if he heard a lie.

Milo leaned against his hands on the bed and sighed. "That day we were supposed to have dinner, Kenji asked to have lunch with me. He fed me fugu and said I should stay away from you. That you deserved better, that you deserved him."

The horror was clear in Kaz's face when he said, "He threatened to poison you?"

"Hey, I wanted to do the same thing to that model earlier." He shrugged.

Kaz backed away from the bed and picked his jacket up off the floor.

"Where are you going?" Milo asked as Kaz made his way to the suite door.

"When I return, I want you to hide in that closet and watch," he said, pausing with his hand on the doorknob.

"I don't understand."

Kaz pinned him with a stern stare. "Just do as I ask."

Milo nodded.

HALF AN hour later, the door to the suite opened once more. Unsure what was going on but not wanting to disobey Kaz, Milo hid in the closet. Two men entered the room, both speaking Nihongo. He immediately recognized them as Kaz and Kenji.

Kaz strode in with that sure stride, shoulders squared, chin held high while Kenji swept in like one of the ladies from old England, all bustle and color. The two men couldn't be any more opposite from one another. Maybe that was what made their friendship work.

Milo held his breath. Good thing he'd picked up after Kaz and tidied the bed. He hated to think what would happen should Kenji suspect another person waited in the shadows.

A jovial air floated between the longtime friends and business partners. Kenji murmured something that Milo didn't hear, but the full-bodied laugh from Kaz that followed seemed to reach into Milo's body and grip his heart. He left the closet door slightly ajar so he could see into the bedroom all the way to the living room.

Kaz moved out of sight to another part of the suite as Kenji folded himself onto one of the cream couches like a flower in full bloom. The distinctive pop of a cork surprised a laugh out of the designer.

It seemed Kaz had opened the champagne bottle that arrived ten minutes before they had. Then he returned with two champagne flutes filled three-fourths of the way with the bubbling golden liquid. Confusion covered Milo in its suffocating embrace.

He handed one to Kenji, who smiled up at him as he accepted the glass. The adoration on his face made Milo's stomach lurch. How Kaz had remained ignorant of the other man's feelings escaped understanding when the obvious stared him in the face.

"To your success," Kaz said, touching the lip of his glass to Kenji's.

"To *our* success," Kenji revised before taking a sip. He licked the corner of his lips and deposited his glass onto the coffee table. "To be honest, I thought I wouldn't see you at the gala again after you left with that… *assistant.*"

The loaded pause pinched a nerve. Milo gritted his teeth to keep from cursing. He needed to trust that Kaz had some sort of plan, because making him sit and watch what played out was cruel and unusual punishment. *Assistant my ass.*

Kaz settled his long limbs onto the opposite couch. "That assistant happens to work for one of the most powerful women in fashion."

"Cassandra knows I'm more valuable to her than she is to me." Kenji rested his temple on one pointy fingernail. How it didn't puncture skin baffled Milo. "*Rebel* isn't the only magazine wanting an exclusive with me."

"I see." Kaz laid his ankle over one knee and stretched his arms over the back of the couch. "I'd like to think that you've always wanted what was best for me. Isn't that right? I certainly wanted that for you. Always."

The air between them shifted slightly. Milo felt it in the sweat that began to gather at his fingertips.

Kenji tilted his head. In Nihongo, he said, "Where is this coming from? You know that all I want is for you to be happy. I've got your back."

A pensive expression came over Kaz's handsome features. "There were so many years when I only had you."

Milo's heart clenched. Jealousy pinched at the most delicate parts of him.

"You will always have me, Yuki-kun."

The intimacy of the conversation made Milo feel like a voyeur. Like he was intruding on a private moment. Like he shouldn't be there for this.

"I beg to differ."

Kenji shifted. "What makes you think otherwise?"

"Did you think I wouldn't find out?" he asked, maintaining his cool control.

"Find out about what?" Kenji asked, taking another sip from his glass.

"That you threatened Milo? Asked him to break up with me?"

A shiver ran down Milo's spine at the cruelty in Kaz's voice. Never did he want to be on the receiving end of that tone. It surprised him that Kenji still managed to breathe evenly, faced with such potent hostility.

"But he doesn't deserve you," Kenji said, sliding his glass onto the coffee table between them.

"And you do?"

"Kazuhiko—"

Kaz lifted a hand and interrupted Kenji. "In many ways, you saved me from a life full of so much cruelty and pain. You know me more than most, yet now I realize that you've never known my heart."

"I saved you more times than I'd care to count," Kenji said, leaning forward. "I healed your wounds inside and out."

"And for that I am grateful."

"Kazuhiko, no koto ga daisuki."

Milo sucked in a breath. His hand flew to his mouth to muffle his shock. Kenji did it. He actually told Kaz how he felt.

The sadness that rained over Kaz lasted but a moment. "That doesn't give you license to threaten someone important to me."

"What does he have that I don't?" Kenji demanded, his voice rising. "I've known you all my life. I've been there for you. What has he done for you?"

The corner of Kaz's lips twitched up in an almost imperceptible smile. Unfortunately, Kenji caught the emotion before Kaz could hide it.

The designer pushed to his feet. "You have to let me at least try. You owe me that much."

"I owe you nothing. Not after what you've done."

Kenji's jaw dropped. "You don't mean that. All these years of friendship—"

"Let me put this to rest," Kaz said like a judge handing down a verdict. "I simply do not share the same feelings for you."

"No!"

The screech pierced Milo's ears. He refused to watch any longer.

CHAPTER TWENTY-TWO
BANISHMENT

MAKING HIS decision, Milo pushed the closet door aside and stepped out. "Stop!"

Kenji whipped his head around and hissed, "You! You did this."

Angry tears welled up in Kenji's eyes. Milo looked from him to Kaz, who stayed seated.

"What Kenji did was wrong," Milo continued. "But humiliating him won't change anything. He is already broken. I know. My love for Celeste pretty much destroyed me."

"Are you sure about this?" Kaz asked.

"Do I approve of what he did?" Milo shook his head. "But I'm man enough to move on."

Milo rounded the couch, ignoring the hissing Kenji—mascara running down his face—to sit beside Kaz. He placed a hand on Kaz's chest, felt the powerful beat of the heart beneath, and looked into his eyes.

"Am I still yours?" he asked.

Kaz tilted Milo's chin up and placed a chaste kiss on his lips. "Hai."

"Good." Milo thumped Kaz's chest with his open palm. "Because you are as much mine as I am yours."

Desire sparked within those blue eyes and called to Milo's own need. If Kenji wasn't watching, Milo was sure they would be horizontal on the floor with no clothes on.

"So how do you think it makes me feel that you're crushing another man's spirit before my eyes?" Milo asked, serious as hell.

"I was trying to—"

"I know what you were trying to do," he interrupted. "Thank you for that. If you want to end your friendship with Kenji, that's your choice. Either way, you have me." He stared straight into Kaz's eyes. "You have *all* of me."

"Do you honestly think you will get away with this?" Kenji spat, trying for some semblance of control. He flipped his hair back and sniffed. "Our deal is off."

"I don't care what you do," Milo said, turning to face him but keeping his hand on Kaz's chest. The contact was a steadying force for him, and at the back of his mind, he knew it was the same for Kaz. "If you want, I will even give you Cassandra's room number so you can visit her tonight. But I wouldn't advise that, because she's probably with someone and wouldn't appreciate being disturbed." He smirked. "You'll have to wait until morning to pull your exclusive, but I will leave you with this question. How do you think it will look to the other magazines if you suddenly pull out of what is essentially a major contract?"

"Have you seen my show?" Kenji raised an eyebrow. "Everyone loves me."

"Oh, they do." Milo nodded. "And I have no doubt you'll land on your feet. But the fashion industry has a long memory. Being on the wrong side of *Rebel*... of Cassandra? Do you honestly think that's the best thing for a rising star to do?"

Kenji opened his mouth, but no words came out. Milo saw the wheels turning in his head. He was making mental calculations.

"The fashion world may forgive you," Kaz finally said. "But I never will."

"Kazuhiko," Kenji gasped out. "You seriously can't be considering that—" He waved at Milo as if he were nothing but a piece of trash along the road. "—over me, can you?"

"After all our years of friendship, I would think you should know me better than that." Kaz snaked his arm around Milo's waist and pulled him closer until Milo was nestled against him. "You know what I have been through. You know what has been taken from me. What it took for me to get where I am today."

Kenji squirmed, dropping his gaze as if there were nothing more fascinating than the orchid pattern of his kimono. "Don't be like that."

"You would take away my happiness too? Then you are no better than my family."

At that statement, Milo and Kenji gasped in unison. Milo had no idea what the designer was shocked about, but he couldn't believe what he was hearing.

"I make you happy?" he stammered.

"More than you know." Kaz kissed his forehead but then returned his gaze to Kenji. "As of today, I am cutting off your hemp supply."

"Yuki-kun!" Kenji's voice reached such heights that Milo feared for the integrity of all the glass in the room.

The shift wasn't lost on Milo either. Like a thread snapping, something indeed ended between Kaz and Kenji that night. A part of Milo couldn't help but feel responsible.

"You will have to find another source," Kaz continued, using a more official tone. It was like he were handing down a decree from the heavens. "Although I doubt you will find better quality than what I have been supplying. And with legal means."

"Please don't do this." Kenji finally managed to stand, but he wobbled. "You're effectively ending my career."

"You crossed a line. Milo may find it in his heart to forgive you, but I cannot. You are dead to me." The last part Kaz said in Nihongo, which carried more weight.

Heartbreak was clear on Kenji's face as a fresh wave of tears streamed down his cheeks. He covered his trembling lips with the back of his hand. Backing away, he reached the door in five steps. Then he spun on his heel and left the room in a billow of silk.

The moment the door closed, Kaz turned Milo around to face him. He opened his mouth as if to say something, and Milo waited with bated breath. Instead, Kaz leaned down until their foreheads met. Then he inhaled deeply. His exhale tickled Milo's slightly parted lips.

"Thank you for stopping me," Kaz whispered, his shoulders falling as the last of the tension left the air around them. "I don't know what I would have said if you hadn't."

"What made you think humiliating him was the right thing to do?" Milo asked, his shoulders relaxing too.

"I wasn't thinking. All I wanted was to show him that he didn't inspire those feelings in me." When Kaz shook his head, their foreheads rubbed together. "I was so angry. That he hurt you. That I couldn't be with you. Kenji has hinted at his feelings before, but I never felt the same for him. This is the first time that he's actually come out and said it."

"But are you sure?" Milo looked Kaz in the eyes again. "What you said earlier. You two seem like you've gone through a lot. Being with me doesn't mean you have to end years of friendship."

As if he couldn't stand not having Milo close, Kaz pulled him into his arms and rested his chin on top of Milo's head. "I don't want someone in my life who is capable of hurting those I care about. I know you and I have a long way to go, but I will not stop pursuing you to the ends of the earth and back. I promise you that."

A chuckle burst out of Milo. "We can't even sit through an entire dinner together."

"I want to remedy that."

"I fly home to New York tomorrow."

Kaz cursed under his breath. "I have a few more things to take care of here."

"I'm starting to get a feeling this dinner will never happen."

Lifting a finger for silence, Kaz fished out his cellphone and dialed a number from memory. In rapid-fire Nihongo, he cleared his schedule on Friday of the coming week and booked a reservation at one of the most exclusive gentleman's clubs in the city.

"You're a member of the Hellfire Club?" Milo whistled. "I shouldn't be surprised, but I am."

"My grandfather on my mother's side was."

"You're a legacy." A corner of Milo's lips tugged up. "Figures."

Kaz ended the call and pocketed his phone. In one smooth movement, he stood up from the couch and pulled Milo with him. Then he eased Milo onto one of the wingback chairs, where Milo sat without resistance.

At the confusion on his face, Kaz said, "It's taking all of my control not to ravage you here and now. But I don't want to ruin your first time with me with the idea that not ten minutes ago my former best friend confessed his feelings for me."

Milo grimaced at the idea. It was certainly a huge turn-off.

"But," Kaz continued, getting on his knees between Milo's legs, "you have to at least let me take care of this." He ran his fingers over the bulge in Milo's pants.

It was all Milo could do not to buck off the chair at the touch. "You don't have to."

"But I do."

The sound of Milo's zipper being pulled down practically drowned out the hammering of his heart. Kaz reached into the folds of fabric and freed Milo's erection from the constriction. Milo sighed in relief.

Kaz used his thumb to spread the white pearl of precome over the head while he wrapped the rest of his fingers around Milo's engorged shaft. "I've missed the way you taste."

Milo stared at him through hooded eyes and then licked his lips. "I've missed you too."

A moan ripped out of him the second Kaz lowered his head and took all of Milo's length into his mouth. He threw his head back in pure ecstasy at the first glide of Kaz's tongue up his dick.

Then Kaz said, "Look at me while I suck you."

The request was so compelling that Milo lifted his head and dropped his gaze on his penis. He shoved his fingers through Kaz's jet-black hair and said, "Swallow every last bit of my come."

A grin that was enough to melt the polar icecaps manifested along Kaz's lips before he resumed his careful ministrations. Milo moved his hand to the back of Kaz's head. Unabashedly, he lifted his hips, slamming himself deeper. Kaz didn't mind. In fact, he swallowed repeatedly every time the head of Milo's cock reached the back of his throat.

The pleasure was exquisite, unlike anything Milo had ever felt in his life.

"That's it," he said. "Fuck me with your mouth."

Kaz met his gaze. The blue of his irises was pretty much swallowed entirely by black. His desire was a tangible thing. Milo could almost taste it, which only served to take his pleasure to new heights.

He swiveled his hips as Kaz hollowed out his cheeks. Then, when Kaz's head bobbed down again, he took Milo's balls into his hand and gave them a swift tug. Milo grunted, his ass clenching.

Never had he felt so empty there. It was as if everything in him wanted Kaz to ride him until they both couldn't stand. But that could wait.

Milo focused all of his being on the heat of Kaz's mouth and what his talented tongue was doing. It seemed like forever since he had come. And the moment the thought of release hit him, he felt the pressure build until he plunged one last time into Kaz's mouth and exploded.

As commanded, Kaz swallowed every last drop, maintaining eye contact the entire time. Milo lost all feeling on everything south of his waist as he slumped into the chair. That was probably the best head of his life, he thought as he panted some life back into his body.

Kaz sat back onto his haunches, a boyish grin on his handsome face. "You should go before I change my mind and take you where you sit."

"Give me a minute," Milo said, equally grinning. "I don't think I can move."

"You're welcome."

"Arrogant ass."

Without warning, Kaz grabbed Milo's buttocks and pulled him forward. A yelp escaped Milo before Kaz shoved his tongue into Milo's mouth. He melted into the kiss, tasting the salt of his body on Kaz. A primal need called for more, much more.

But just as Milo was getting into the kiss, Kaz pulled back, righted his clothes and then Milo's, and lifted him into his arms.

"What are you doing?" Milo asked in surprise, breathless.

"I'm taking you back to your hotel. What does it look like I'm doing?"

"You can't seriously carry me all the way!"

"You said you couldn't move."

"If you give me a minute—"

"If I give you any longer than a few seconds, I won't have any control left." He pinned Milo with a meaningful stare. "It's been a tough night on all of us."

CHAPTER TWENTY-THREE
BREAK

MILO WALKED on air into the office Monday morning. All in all—despite his near catatonic state—Paris Fashion Week was a smashing success. He returned with no less than a dozen suits from both top and up-and-coming designers, several pairs of shoes, silk ties, and a kilt for some reason, which he had no idea what to do with. Maybe Tommy might like it as a thank-you gift for his help at the gala.

A part of Milo still felt guilty over spurning his friend's feelings. Regardless of what Tommy said about trying a monogamous relationship, Milo doubted Tommy's fortitude. And their friendship meant too much to him. He preferred they dance around each other awkwardly for a few months than lose what they'd shared for several years.

Yet another part of Milo wanted to give in to his curiosity. There was no doubt of Tommy's prowess in the bedroom... and wherever else he liked to fuck. Milo attended several parties where other models bragged about Tommy's stamina and creativity.

But Milo's curiosity remained just that. He already had Kaz, and he had no doubt of Kaz's skills—if Milo went by his dexterous tongue alone. So it was no surprise that Milo found it hard to concentrate on work the entire week.

Anticipation mounted for their Friday dinner and what would happen afterward. It didn't help that Kaz sent him flowers every day, to the point where Milo had to give away some of the vases because his desk was full. The naughty texts and phone sex exacerbated matters.

It seemed with each minute that passed, Milo grew hornier and hornier. Surviving dinner without jumping Kaz's bones there and then seemed like a farfetched concept.

But the Hellfire Club?

Even Milo hadn't been to the super secretive, super exclusive men's club. Only sons or grandsons of former members were allowed access. Archibald had been given an invitation, but damn his father for declining. Instead, he created his own club, which was located a few miles outside the city.

At his desk Friday afternoon, Milo pushed away thoughts of his father and kept himself busy while he waited for Cassandra to return from lunch. He refused to count down the minutes until Jiro arrived in front of their building to pick him up.

Behind him hung a garment bag with one of the suits that had come home with him from Paris. In many ways, that night was their first date.

All morning, since Kaz arrived in the city, they had exchanged text messages like teenagers. At one point he called, and Milo almost dropped his phone. The conversation had to be quick, since Milo was headed into a meeting with marketing, but he had blushed ever since.

The phone at his desk beeped, and Milo picked up the receiver on the first ring. It was the personal assistant of the actress on the cover of their October issue, confirming the time of the shoot. He rattled off the information that was requested just as the elevator doors opened and Cassandra stepped out. He reached for the stack of messages that had arrived while she was gone and prepared himself for their afternoon briefing, giving the call half his attention.

"In my office, now," Cassandra said as she passed.

Milo ended the call and quickly stood up, tablet in hand. He hurried in after her and closed the door behind him.

"Is it true that Kenji tried to poison you?" she asked without preamble. "Was that why you didn't come back to work the day of your lunch with him?"

Milo's jaw dropped. He stood in shocked silence.

A deep furrow formed between Cassandra's eyebrows as she waited for a response. In the back of his mind, he made a mental note to remind her of her Botox appointment.

"Well?"

Cassandra's follow-up question knocked Milo back to the present. He rolled his eyes and sighed.

"He didn't try to poison me. More like he was flexing. The real important question here is how did you find out?"

"Yukifumi told me at lunch," she said.

For the second time, Milo's jaw dropped. "But you were having lunch with—"

"I was," she cut him off. "Yukifumi dropped in and we spoke. He told me that he was dissolving his partnership with House of Suzuki and about what Kenji had done."

Right that instant his tablet pinged with an incoming text. *I'm not sorry.* From Kaz.

Milo wanted to be annoyed; he really did. He'd hoped to leave Cassandra out of it, knowing information might eventually reach his mother. That was the last thing he wanted, because there was a remote possibility that through her, his father might find out. It would pretty much be hellfire and brimstone from there. No one harmed that man's son.

"It's old news," he finally said, regaining his composure. "As you can see, Kaz took care of it. You don't have to... what are you doing?"

Cassandra picked up the receiver of the phone on her desk and quickly dialed a number.

After a couple of seconds, she said, "Mandatory meeting. Tell everyone. I am replacing the exclusive on the House of Suzuki. Yes. Yes. I want ideas in an hour. No one goes home until we fill in the gap in the issue."

Milo stared, speechless, as Cassandra ended the call.

"I suggest you get ready," she said, as though she hadn't just ended the career of one of the rising stars of fashion. No magazine in their right mind would touch him after she was through. "We have a lot of work to do. I want suggestions from you too."

He backed out of her office, still stunned.

"I CAN'T believe she actually cut Kenji out of the issue," Milo said as he sliced into his two-inch-thick porterhouse steak with gusto. It was a huge piece of meat, medium rare—just the way he liked it— with a side of the silkiest mashed potatoes he had ever tasted.

It seemed like pedestrian fare for the Hellfire Club on the Upper East Side, but according to Kaz, he could order anything he wanted and the chef would make it. There wasn't a menu at the prestigious men's establishment. Already Milo cursed his father for turning down the invitation to join. He could have been a legacy!

But that wasn't the point.

At the moment Milo was still turning over the series of events that had taken place before he left the office. He was half an hour late because the mandatory meeting ran longer than expected. It forced him to change in the car while Jiro navigated Friday rush-hour traffic.

Kaz forgave him. Technically, he was the one responsible for the emergency meeting and complete overhaul of the next issue, which was scheduled for printing by the end of next week. Not that the *Rebel* staff had never started from scratch before. The spring-dresses debacle of two years back still gave everyone nightmares. Even the mention of it was enough to send all the blood in Milo's body to the soles of his feet.

"I like this editor in chief of yours." Kaz lifted his wineglass to his lips and took a delicate sip.

For a second all Milo did was stare as Kaz's throat worked while he swallowed. Evil naughty thoughts assailed him. Suddenly the piece of steak in his mouth transformed into something else, something far hotter and saltier.

Ashamed at the lewd turn of his thoughts inside such a stuffy place, Milo picked up his wineglass and swallowed a huge gulp. They were the youngest men there. The rest were graying and wrinkled.

Some gave Milo assessing glances, as if they knew whose son he was, while others studied Kaz—they definitely knew who he was.

"You shouldn't have told Cassandra about Kenji," Milo said, pouting. He returned his glass to the table and cut through his steak for the next bite.

Kaz leaned back and studied him closely enough to make Milo want to squirm. Kaz's blue eyes held the same heat he'd shown in Paris while sucking him off. How Milo managed not to spontaneously combust when he arrived was still a mystery.

Did the rest of the room know what Kaz was thinking that very second? Could they feel the electricity arcing in the air between them?

"I thought it best to let her know I will no longer be his partner," Kaz replied casually. "What Kenji had done just happened to slip out during the course of our conversation."

"How did that go? 'And by the way, he fed your employee a potentially lethal substance'?" Milo rolled his eyes.

"Are you mad at me?" Kaz challenged. "Because I'm not above angry sex. Not the plan for your first time, but I'm happy to oblige."

"Shh!" Milo glanced around. "Say that a little louder, why don't you?"

"What? That in less than an hour I plan to fuck you until you cannot walk straight?"

That did it. The heat at the tips of Milo's ears traveled to the rest of his face. He must have been as red as the wine they were drinking.

Kaz threw his head back and laughed. The rich sound drew the attention of everyone within hearing distance. The dining room grew silent as Milo felt all eyes on them.

"Will you stop teasing me? I'm horny enough as it is," he hissed under his breath.

"You have no idea," Kaz said, sobering immediately. "If it wouldn't get us kicked out of this place, I would have you on this table right now. Good thing I don't want an audience. You make the most beautiful face when you come."

Another wave of awareness sent blood rushing from Milo's head down to the throbbing member between his legs. He ached for Kaz's touch, craved it like the air he breathed. The dark paneling of the room seemed to close in around them. The portraits of the distinguished members of the club seemed to condemn the lust riding Milo's body hard.

"I wouldn't be surprised if Kenji was blackballed from the fashion industry by the end of next week," Milo said, returning to their previous conversation in an attempt to keep things civilized for a little while longer.

His mother taught him better, after all. A healthy sex life was all well and good, but not around polite company. Hilarious, since he doubted if half the men in the room with him could still achieve an erection without help.

"It's nothing less than what he deserves," Kaz said, granting Milo a reprieve by softening the desire in his expression.

"But I hate that such a talented designer's career would be ruined. Sure, Kenji threatened to kill me—"

"No one threatens what is mine."

Kaz spoke with so much conviction that it was hard for Milo not to believe him. Would he have done the same if someone threatened Kaz's life?

The thought of losing Kaz was enough to break him, make his blood boil. So yeah, maybe considering drastic measures wasn't above Milo. But what did he really know about Kaz, other than he was a businessman?

They would sleep together that night. It was a foregone conclusion.

"You're ruthless," Milo teased before he leaned forward and said, "I'm yours."

The severity of Kaz's expression eased when he nodded.

"But understand that you are also mine," he continued. Kaz squared his shoulders. Milo felt all of Kaz's attention focus on him. *Good.* "And with that comes certain expectations."

"Like what expectations?" Kaz asked, looking like the calculating businessman Milo knew him to be.

"That you will tell me more about yourself."

Kaz was silent for a long moment. Then he leaned back and rubbed his chin.

What was there to consider? There should be no secrets between them. Anything less was unacceptable.

"I will tell you what you need to know when you need to know," Kaz said.

Milo let go of his fork and knife and sat back as well. If that was how Kaz wanted to play it, then so be it. Better to hammer out the details before they went any further.

"This is not a negotiation," was his equally calm reply.

"Everything is a negotiation," Kaz countered.

"Not in my world." Milo reached for his wineglass and set it on the arm of his chair. He pinched the stem with his thumb and forefinger and began to stroke it up and down. Almost immediately he felt Kaz's gaze shift to what he was doing. "I'm prepared to give you all of me. It is only right that you give me all of you in return. Those are the terms. I want nothing less."

Milo noticed that Kaz regarded him with steely admiration and a hint of humor. "You drive a hard bargain, McLaren-san."

"Take it or leave it, Yukifumi-sama," he teased back.

Then something caught Kaz's attention from behind Milo. In seconds his face went from serious to pale. Concern blossomed in Milo's chest. He was about to turn around to see what was going on when Kaz spoke Nihongo in a less than certain tone.

"What are you doing here?"

CHAPTER TWENTY-FOUR
BOND

ALARMED BY the absolute horror in Kaz's eyes even if his face remained passive, Milo twisted around to see what inspired such a reaction. A few yards away stood a handsome Japanese man in a coal gray suit complete with vest—buttoned up. A well-groomed goatee framed his lips. It gave him a striking appearance.

"You're a hard man to track down, Kazuhiko," he said in Nihongo.

Milo turned back around. "Kaz, do you know him?"

With an almost imperceptible shift in his seat, Kaz relaxed his shoulders and said, "Maybe because I don't want to be found."

"Hiding is futile. You should know this by now. When Father calls, you answer."

Father?

Milo's eyebrows rose as he continued to stare at Kaz, whose shoulders hitched upward at the mention. In this case, *otōsama* had been used, which was a more formal address for someone's parent.

"I'm out." Kaz sneered. "What don't you understand?"

"No one ever gets out." A pause. "Alive. Especially for you and me."

Kaz stiffened once more, and Milo's heart skipped. He was unaware of what the hell was going on, but an air of danger quickly surrounded them. An invisible static seemed to prick all the exposed skin on Milo's body.

"Leave."

The threat in Kaz's voice forced Milo to sit up straighter. If he hadn't known the demand wasn't directed at him, he actually

169

might have gotten to his feet and walked away. He had never seen Kaz so... dangerous.

He knew there was a hidden beast beneath the mask Kaz wore, but he'd had no idea just how sharp its fangs were until that electrically charged moment. It confused him. Worst of all, it turned him on.

"I'm being rude." The new arrival's tone shifted from less threatening to more charming. "Perhaps I will join you."

"No—" Kaz attempted to push to his feet, but something stopped him that Milo hadn't seen—something that happened over Milo's shoulder too quickly to catch even if he turned around.

In seconds a team of servers arrived with a third chair and another place setting. The man who seemed familiar to Milo unbuttoned his suit jacket and sat down.

A glass of scotch neat was placed to his right. He picked it up and downed its entire contents, not stopping to taste what was probably expensive and old. They only served the best of everything at the Hellfire.

A second glass of scotch arrived within seconds of the first, and Milo mourned. It seemed he and Kaz were destined never to finish dinner without interruption. Maybe they should scale down.

Start with lunch... or breakfast. They had at least managed breakfast. With exciting results, he might add.

This time, the man sipped instead of gulped. Apparently he was settling down for the duration. A charismatic grin spread across his face.

The air surrounding Kaz darkened significantly. If Milo believed in auras, he would swear a black mass writhed around him. Gone was the happy, amiable guy who waited patiently for Milo to arrive. What sat in his place was a rabid dog ready to bite at the slightest provocation.

"I'm really not sure what's happening here," Milo said, looking from a clearly distressed Kaz to the man who had crashed their dinner. He reached out a hand to the man. "My name is Milo McLaren, and you are?"

"Let me commend you on your Nihongo," the man said as he shook Milo's hand. "I am Haruhiko Yukifumi. It's a pleasure meeting you."

Every muscle in Milo's body tensed. He wasn't sure if he should be happy or weary. Kaz seemed to be on the defensive.

"Yukifumi." Milo looked to Kaz for confirmation, but he refused to look Milo's way.

"I apologize for my brother," Haruhiko said. "He can be uptight when I'm around. Sibling rivalry and all that."

"I will say this again," Kaz finally said. "Leave."

"Why?" Haruhiko faced him. "It seems like we have a lot to catch up on. How do you know my brother, Milo-san?"

"Please, just Milo."

Haruhiko tipped his head in acknowledgment.

Milo didn't fail to catch the use of *otōto*, which denoted that Kaz was younger. By how many years, Milo couldn't be sure. They seemed close in age, and he finally saw the resemblance.

It was in the eyes and the angles of their cheekbones and jawlines. But where Kaz's eyes were crystal blue, Haruhiko's were bottomless pits of deep onyx. They were unnerving to look at, since the pupils couldn't be distinguished from the irises.

"Kaz and I—"

"Are business acquaintances," Kaz cut him off.

Milo's mouth was left hanging open. After everything they'd shared? That was the most Kaz introduced him as?

Hurt took root in his chest.

"Oh, really?" Haruhiko continued regarding Milo unblinkingly. "In what sector are you in, Milo?"

"Fashion," Kaz answered for him. "We met through Kenji."

"Ah!" The smile that spread through Haruhiko's face unsettled Milo. Apparently snakes could smile. "How is Kenji doing?"

A tense second passed before Kaz said, "Kenji and I have parted ways."

"How unfortunate. I was so looking forward to seeing him." Haruhiko took another sip from his drink and focused once again on

Milo. "But it seems like I walked into something else. How well do you know my brother? Because I have stories—"

Kaz's hand closed around his brother's wrist. The force of it rattled the table's contents, and the clatter startled those within hearing distance.

Angry glares darted their way. But it seemed only Milo was affected by the ire of the room. The brothers Yukifumi merely stared at one another like someone's head was about to come off.

Having had enough, Milo did the one thing he told himself never to do: He channeled his father. He sat up straight and withdrew all emotion from his face until only a cold mask remained. Then he turned his gaze to Kaz. When those blue eyes landed on him, they widened in surprise. Enough to let go of Haruhiko's wrist.

Haruhiko went from staring daggers at his brother to turning to Milo. He swallowed and squared his shoulders as if preparing for a confrontation. Both men waited.

With unhurried movements, Milo picked up his fork and knife and resumed cutting his steak. Once a perfect square piece had been separated from the whole, he brought the fork to his lips and placed the morsel of meat into his mouth.

He chewed slowly, savoring the already cool dish. Then he swallowed and slanted a glance toward Haruhiko. Kaz's older brother shifted slightly.

"I don't know who you are," Milo said in an even tone. "And I will definitely get answers from him." He pointed the tip of his knife toward Kaz. "But as you can see, you are interrupting our dinner. Clearly you have business to settle with your brother. I respect that."

Milo paused. He picked up his wineglass and tipped a fair amount into his mouth.

After he replaced the glass beside his plate, he continued in measured Nihongo, "But do it on your own time."

"Do you honestly think—"

With two raised fingers, Milo cut Haruhiko off. "Does it look like I care what you think?" Then he signaled for one of the servers. "Please see Mr. Yukifumi out."

"But sir—"

The server's protest died as soon as Milo's gaze landed on him.

"No need," Haruhiko said, regaining his composure. He finished the rest of his scotch and pushed his chair away from the table. With deft fingers, he buttoned his suit jacket and tugged at the cuffs of his shirt. "We will speak again soon, Kazuhiko. It was a pleasure meeting you, McLaren-san."

The switch to formality sounded more like a warning than a show of respect. Milo tilted his head slightly and glanced up at Haruhiko.

"Until we meet again."

And with those four words, Kaz's brother weaved his way between tables and left the dining room.

As soon as he was gone, Milo closed his eyes and let out a long breath. With all his might, he pushed back the monster he'd locked away so many years ago. When he was sure he was himself again, he opened his eyes.

"Who was that?" Kaz asked, switching back to English, his shock evident in his expression.

"Someone you will never want to see ever again." Milo frowned. "What the hell was all that? You never told me you had a brother. And he seems like such a delight."

The sarcasm in Milo's voice didn't produce the humor he hoped to achieve. Instead, Kaz sat back in his chair and ordered something stronger than wine. When his drink arrived—scotch, just like his brother—he downed the entire glass in one swig. Also like his brother. It was unsettling.

"Haruhiko and I share a father but not a mother," Kaz said after he swallowed. "He is the firstborn. Unfortunately, I am the favorite, and he sees that as a threat. So, to keep the peace, I left Japan."

Milo blinked several times. It was too much information to take in all at once. Never had Kaz spoken so candidly about himself.

"Then what is he doing here?" he managed to ask when his brain finally processed everything.

Sibling rivalries weren't uncommon, especially in Japan where excellence was valued. Kaz was a businessman, and from the looks of it, his brother might be too.

"Haruhiko is loyal to a fault." Kaz sighed. "He may hate every fiber of my being and curse the day I was born—"

"You're being a tad overdramatic, don't you think?" Milo interrupted, hoping to lighten the mood.

From the way Kaz shook his head, that attempt hadn't worked either.

"My brother being here means that my father wants me back in Japan." Kaz rubbed his lips. "And that's the last thing I want."

"Then don't go."

"If only it were that simple."

"The way I see it, your life is here now. You have a business here. I'm here. If you don't want to go home, then you don't have to."

"I'm sorry for earlier."

"Earlier?"

"For calling you my business associate. I wanted to claim you, but I was afraid that if I did, Haruhiko would use it to harm you in some way."

The hurt that had blossomed in Milo's chest earlier disappeared. He reached across the table and squeezed Kaz's hand. Kaz intertwined their fingers together and brought their locked hands up to his lips. He placed a kiss on Milo's knuckles and then pressed his cheek against the place his lips had been.

"I can take care of myself," Milo said. "In case you forgot, I'm the one who drove your brother out of here."

Kaz pinned him with a serious look. "As alluring as I find that little performance of yours, I believe it only served to antagonize Haruhiko. It was a strategic retreat."

"You're honestly not saying we may have won the battle…."

"But not the war," Kaz finished for him. "That's exactly it."

"That's taking things a little too far, isn't it?" Milo took back his hand.

As much as he wanted to keep holding on to Kaz, a chill ran down his spine. He was afraid that Kaz might feel his palm grow clammy. It had been a long time since he had felt that way—unsure, unsafe, defensive.

"I honestly don't know. But I will not rest until I get to the bottom of why he is really here. It has to be more than just my father sending him to retrieve me."

"Why am I sensing our plans tonight are over?"

Kaz gave him an apologetic look. "Jiro will drive you home."

"I can take a cab."

"For my own peace of mind, let Jiro drive you."

Milo slumped back. "I'm starting to think that we are cursed never to have an uninterrupted dinner."

Pushing his chair back, Kaz stood and made his way to Milo's side of the table. He bent down and whispered into Milo's ear, "Just because we can't finish dinner doesn't mean we can't have dessert later."

And just like that, dinner interrupted or not, Milo's lust returned.

CHAPTER TWENTY-FIVE
BLINDING

AN HOUR later, Milo came home to an empty apartment. He paused at the entrance and closed his eyes. Not a sound. The air smelled stale—like no one had been in the space for hours.

Tommy had left two days earlier for Santorini and the Ralph Lauren summer shoot. He imagined himself transported to the black beaches of the famous Greek island and breathing in the salty Aegean air. Then Kaz entered the daydream in black board shorts and with a sexy grin.

A groan slipped out of Milo. He had been torturing himself all night since Kaz left the Hellfire Club to deal with his brother.

Kaz had a brother. From another mother. Someone who seemed dangerous in a sick, calculating sort of way.

It had been a long time since Milo was in the presence of a man like that. Dealing with that type was never easy. He shuddered when unwanted memories replaced the beach and Kaz and cocktails.

He might not know much about Kaz, but the sharing of personal history went both ways. Kaz knew the Milo who worked at *Rebel*, the Milo who had his heart broken by Celeste. Kaz had no idea who Milo was before all that—the Milo who lived in the kingdom his tyrannical father had built out of concrete mixed with blood. The monster he let out for the briefest second to get rid of an equally menacing beast.

Men like Haruhiko only responded to dominance. Assert it and they backed down. Milo had pegged him the instant he twisted in his chair to face him.

The weight of grocery bags in each hand reminded Milo that he'd bought ice cream.

As soon as he got into the town car waiting at the curb outside the Hellfire, he asked Jiro to take him to the nearest supermarket. He figured he might as well get some of the weekly grocery shopping done before he headed home.

Milo made his way to the kitchen and deposited the bags on the counter. The ice cream went into the freezer first, and then he sorted the rest of the items. Kaz had promised dessert, but Milo lowered his expectations for anything more that night. Haruhiko seemed like the kind of guy who didn't take no for an answer. So much like Kaz in that sense.

When the groceries were put away, Milo tugged off his tie and headed for the bathroom for a nice hot shower to relax tense muscles. Then it was off to bed.

THOUGHTS OF the beach followed Milo into his dreams. He lay on a white lounge chair with the softest cushions. A large umbrella shielded him from the hot kiss of the sun. A cool breeze caressed his bare chest while he sipped from a tart-and-sweet cocktail that mirrored a sunset in a bulbous glass.

Sunglasses shielded his eyes from the glare of the blue water beneath the clear sky. He should really be working on his tan, but he had no one to rub SPF on his skin to keep him from crisping.

Then, like James Bond in *Casino Royale*, Kaz emerged from the waves. He flipped his head back, and water jumped in an arch behind him. When he shook his head, it seemed like the movement was in slow motion.

Milo sat up from his relaxed position and pulled off his sunglasses. He had to squint from the sudden brightness, but it wasn't enough to blind him to the delectable creature wading out of the water.

Droplets created trails down Kaz's chest, crawling over the swell of his abs. Kaz was cut, his definition mouthwatering. Milo swallowed.

He was thirsty for more than the cocktail in his hand. The way the black board shorts rode low on Kaz's hips should be considered illegal. And the *V* that the end of his torso created? It was enough to send all the blood in Milo's body south of the border.

Making eye contact, Kaz ran his fingers through his wet hair. The strands pulled back from his handsome face, exposing all those sharp lines and angles. His lips quirked up in that sexy grin Milo was powerless against. His breathing hitched with every step Kaz took toward him.

"What are you doing here?" Milo blurted out when Kaz stood beneath the shade of the umbrella. He smelled of salt and that spicy musk of his body wash, which shouldn't be possible considering he just left the ocean.

"I'm here for you," Kaz said in that deep, sonorous voice of his that never failed to send tingles down Milo's spine. "Are you ready for me?"

All Milo could do was nod like an idiot. Words failed him. And from the thoughts running around in his head, words weren't needed for what he wanted.

As if reading his filthy mind, Kaz sat on the edge of the lounge chair and pushed Milo back so he was lying down again. Then he leaned in and claimed Milo's waiting mouth.

Kaz thrust the tip of his tongue between the seam of Milo's lips. He took advantage of Milo's moan and plunged his tongue in, deepening the kiss.

Kaz tasted of burnt apples and lust. Milo wrapped his arms around Kaz's shoulders and pulled him down until their chests touched. He raked his fingers through Kaz's still-damp hair. The strands were cool against Milo's overheated skin.

He wanted more, needed more, so he pouted and growled his displeasure when Kaz pulled back. Their gazes met for a hot second before Kaz trailed kisses down Milo's neck. He threw his head back to give Kaz better access.

At the base of the column, where Milo's pulse hammered, Kaz used his teeth. The pleasure-pain of the bite startled Milo enough to arch away from the lounge chair. He felt it all the way to his rigid erection.

Gasping, Milo opened his eyes to his darkened room. Gone was the bright sunlit beach, but the solid body on top of him remained.

"Kaz?" he asked in a sleepy voice. "How did you get in? I know I locked the door."

"You really need to consider moving to another apartment. The security here is appalling." Lips touched Milo's ear before the words, "I bribed your building manager to let me in."

Kaz cupped Milo's dick over his pajama bottoms. His hips jerked up, wanting more of the friction Kaz's large hand provided.

"Your brother?" he managed to ask before all coherent thoughts scattered.

"He's the last thing you should be thinking about while I'm on top of you." Kaz removed his hand and bulk from Milo's body, leaving him bereft.

"Where are you going?" Milo sat up, panic beginning at the center of his chest.

In the gloom he barely made out Kaz shrugging off his suit jacket. Then he reached for the bedside lamp and flicked the switch. The soft light blinded Milo for a second, but with each blink to clear his vision it seemed that more of Kaz's clothes joined his jacket on the chair in the corner.

Not once did Kaz turn his back on Milo. His hands made quick work of the buttons along his crisp white shirt. The instant his chest was exposed, Milo's throat closed. Reality was a hundred times better.

"You were dreaming about me," Kaz said, wicked humor in his tone.

There was no use denying it. "When don't I ever?"

"What was I doing in your dream?"

Milo told him about the beach and the beginnings of an awesome make-out session with the hope of more. With each description, the heat in Kaz's blue eyes intensified. Milo couldn't help but follow

179

Kaz's hands when he reached to unclasp the belt around his waist. In a swift tug, the leather band was gone, left to fall to the floor.

"You're seriously going to leave the light on?" Milo asked, his prudish side resurfacing.

"I want to see your face when you come," Kaz said matter-of-factly. He undid his pants, let them fall, and stepped out of the pool of black fabric.

The front of his boxer briefs was already straining when he stepped closer to Milo's bed. Then, on all fours, he crawled toward Milo until their lips touched. Like in the dream, Milo opened for Kaz's tongue. But, unlike the dream, Kaz curled his hands around the hem of Milo's shirt. Instead of pulling up, he pulled on opposite ends and rent the fabric like it was tissue paper.

"Did you really have to do that?" Milo asked, looking down at his ruined shirt.

"I'll buy you ten more."

"Sure, because that's what this is about."

Kaz smirked and then cupped the back of Milo's neck and pulled him forward. The searing kiss made up for the torn shirt, which he easily shrugged out of. Kaz eased Milo onto his back and trailed kisses down his neck.

"Dreams really do come true," Milo said in a happy gasp as Kaz bit down on the pulse at the base of his neck.

"For what I have planned for you?" Kaz licked one puckered nipple and squeezed the nub between his thumb and forefinger. "Dreams won't be able to compare."

Milo groaned. His back arched off the bed as Kaz focused on the other nipple and gave it the same attention as the first. Rolling both sensitive points between his expert fingers, he traced a line from the center of Milo's chest to his navel with his tongue and plunged the tip into the depression.

Never had Milo known the place to be such an erogenous zone for him. It sent electricity all the way to his toes.

When his nipples were released, Milo took a moment to catch his breath. Kaz hooked his thumbs into the waistband of Milo's pajama bottoms and tugged the fabric down his legs. A sigh of relief escaped Milo's throat.

"I honestly thought you were going to rip those too," he said lazily. "They are my favorite pair."

Instead of responding, Kaz growled. A smirk stretched over Milo's kiss-swollen lips. He hadn't worn anything underneath. It left his cock free for whatever Kaz planned.

"You were waiting for me," Kaz said in wonder.

"I'm always waiting for you" came Milo's impatient reply.

As if hearing the call of Milo's body, Kaz closed his hand around the engorged length. As he stroked, he leaned forward and claimed Milo's lips once more.

Milo took advantage of their close proximity to plunge his hand into Kaz's boxer briefs, and Kaz groaned the instant Milo began to rub his length. They matched each other's rhythm with both their hands and their tongues.

"You are so hot," Milo said between wet kisses. "So big. I want you in me, now."

"So bossy." Kaz chuckled but tightened his grip on the base of Milo's cock, making him yelp in surprise. "Turn around."

As Milo shifted onto his stomach, he said, "Lube and condoms are in the dresser."

The sound of the drawer sliding open was almost as loud as the pounding of Milo's heart. It was really happening. The rip of a condom packet affirmed his thought. The cap of the lube flipping open made him gasp, and he lifted his hips in anticipation, presenting his eager ass to Kaz's ministrations.

With two coated fingers, Kaz circled Milo's entrance. "You should see yourself right now. Puckering for me."

"Kaz," Milo moaned, gripping the sheets. "I want you."

Kaz's large body hovered over his as he whispered, "You have a hungry little ass, don't you? Hot. Tight."

He emphasized the word by slipping in first one finger, then two. Milo's back bowed at the intrusion. The stretch was fire, but he knew that Kaz's girth was more than just two fingers.

The expectation was enough to choke him, so he relaxed into the preparation and felt himself loosen with each stroke. Kaz heightened the sensation by reaching around and running the tip of his finger over the slit of Milo's dick. Then he spread the pearl of precome over the head. Milo thrust forward then back, unsure which sensation he liked best.

Just as Milo reached the edge of his control, Kaz released his cock and pulled his fingers out. But before Milo could protest, Kaz's body covered his again. Then the head of Kaz's dick pushed against Milo's entrance.

A groan of pleasure slipped out of Milo, but the sound was cut off when Kaz paused, only the head inside.

"Kaz," Milo growled. "What are you doing?"

"What do you want me to do?" he asked, sending Milo's frustration into overdrive.

Without responding, Milo reached behind them until his hand closed around one of Kaz's asscheeks. Once he was sure of his grip, he pushed back with his body while he pulled Kaz closer. The move forced Kaz to penetrate him halfway.

They both moaned.

Milo had been both right and wrong—right because Kaz was indeed huge, but wrong because the stretch was more than he thought he could take. It was overwhelming and made him light-headed.

"*Baka*," Kaz gasped, just as breathless. "I don't want to hurt you."

"You won't," Milo lied through his teeth. But with each deep breath, he felt his body relax against the intrusion. "I knew you were big, but this…. So hot. So… good. Quit the bullshit and make me come already."

The command was forceful enough that no other words were necessary. Kaz gripped Milo's hips and pushed in the rest of the way.

A strangled yelp.

Milo wasn't sure if it came from him, but he didn't have time to process the rest of his emotions, because Kaz pulled all the way out until only the tip of his cock remained and then slammed back in. The force was enough to send Milo sprawling over the bed, gripping the sheets for dear life.

The friction of his cock rubbing against the mattress added to the sensation of Kaz filling him to the brim. The stretch was intense, mind-blowing, enough to shatter him to pieces.

Their grunts and moans blended together until Milo was no longer sure who was making which sound. And the slap of skin against skin was maddening. Kaz reverted to Nihongo and spoke dirty words into Milo's ear, turning him on even more.

The pressure built and built in him with each powerful thrust. The friction was more than enough and burned white-hot within him, but Kaz had other plans. He reached around them and began to pump Milo's cock in time with his thrusts. It sent all the nerve endings in Milo's body into overdrive.

Like a flash of lightning, Milo felt his release from the base of his spine. Almost at the same moment, Kaz found his own release. They bowed into each other as Kaz rode out their shared orgasm and Milo milked him for all he was worth.

Milo bucked once, twice, and then collapsed onto the bed. Instead of collapsing on top of him as he expected, Kaz pulled out, panting. Then he flipped Milo over.

With hooded eyes, Milo watched Kaz remove the spent condom and put on a new one. Even after just coming, he was still hard. The man was a machine. He lifted one of Milo's legs over his shoulder and entered him again.

Milo gasped.

"You thought we were done?" Kaz teased, pushing in further until Milo took him to the hilt.

"I never expected anything less."

CHAPTER TWENTY-SIX
BLISS

THE NEXT morning Milo dozed in bed like a contented cat while Kaz showered. At first Milo was tempted to join him, but he wasn't sure he had another orgasm left in him. He was utterly spent—all languid limbs and lazy bones.

Since losing his virginity at the tender age of fourteen, sex was never a sprint for Milo. He had learned to savor the foreplay as much as the main event. But with Kaz? Sex was a fucking marathon, pun intended.

He lost count of how many times he came and in how many positions. As soon as he thought they were done for the night, Kaz shifted him into another sexual act straight out of the *Kama Sutra*. The guy was an insatiable machine.

Milo had never been so thoroughly used in his life. Yet a part of him was ready and willing to go another round... well, maybe in a couple of hours. He was sore in places and had pulled muscles he'd forgotten his body possessed.

"How can you be upright right now?" he mumbled as soon as he heard Kaz's confident steps into the room.

"By sheer force of will," came the reply in the masculine voice that sent shivers all over Milo's body. "If I didn't have to make sure Haruhiko left the country today, I would be in that bed thinking of more ways to make you scream my name."

"There's more?" Milo rolled onto his stomach and stretched. "I honestly think you broke my cock last night, not to mention my ass."

Then Milo opened his eyes and groaned, feeling what should have been his broken dick stir back to life.

"How the hell do you make putting on cufflinks look so damn sexy?" Milo asked.

He rested his cheek on a fist and openly stared at Kaz, already mostly dressed. All that was left was his tie and jacket.

Kaz smirked, but it quickly disappeared the instant he turned to fully face Milo. An all-too-familiar heat returned in those blue depths.

"I like seeing you this way," he said.

"Which way?" Milo shifted to his side and ran his hand down his torso, stopping right at his hip.

"Soft from sex and smelling like me."

Tempted to wrap a hand around his already fully aroused cock, Milo pushed to his feet instead. He crossed the room and picked up Kaz's tie along the way, aware that Kaz's eyes were on him the entire time. When he was standing right in front of Kaz, he lifted his collar and swung the tie over his broad shoulders.

With a grin, Milo said, "I wonder which is faster? You making me come with your hands or me tying this around your neck?" He gave the expensive blue silk a tug.

"Challenge accepted." Kaz wrapped his hand around Milo's penis and began pumping from root to tip, making sure to apply pressure at the base.

Milo bit his lip to keep the moan in. It was insane to start the game when his legs barely supported his weight, the muscles having turned to jelly hours ago. Oh, but what a great game it was.

KAZ LEFT Milo a useless lump—the loser of the necktie challenge—and Milo spent the rest of the morning in bed, taking the longest nap in history. The next time he opened his eyes, the sunlight slanting into his bedroom was orange, and his stomach growled in protest. All that sex burned its fair share of calories.

Still half-asleep, basking in the afterglow, Milo shrugged on a robe and padded his way to the kitchen. There had to be some leftovers in the fridge. He certainly didn't have the strength to wait around for delivery.

The second he rounded the corner—rubbing the last sleep from his eyes—he found several Chinese takeout boxes on the counter and Tommy barefoot. The simple shirt hugged his biceps, and his distressed jeans emphasized his long legs.

"I thought you wouldn't be back until tomorrow," Milo said.

What he should have said was "Thank you for saving my ass from starvation." But Tommy's presence in their apartment was certainly a bigger surprise.

"From the looks of things, you and that Japanese guy finally fucked," said Tommy, a smirk on his sexy lips.

"Will you ever call him by his first name?" Milo rolled his eyes, took a spring roll, and stuffed the entire thing into his mouth. It was hot, but he didn't care. The hunger won.

"Not when he's with the man I love."

Milo coughed into a fist, choking on the remnants of the roll. He swallowed several times and cleared his throat before he could find the voice to speak again.

"Tommy." Milo sighed. "I thought we were already through this."

"Clearly, we're not."

Apparently, it was possible to lose one's appetite despite being half dead with hunger. Milo stepped away from the counter and tugged the robe tighter around his body until he was crossing his arms.

"What do you want from me?" Milo asked.

"I already told you what I want." Tommy raked his fingers through his hair. Then he inhaled deeply and exhaled slowly. Once the breath was spent, he said, "It's obvious you have feelings for him. It's also obvious that I have feelings for you."

"Do you want me to move out?"

"Where the hell did that question come from?"

The confusion on Tommy's face took Milo aback. "If my being with Kaz is painful for you, then I'm willing to move out. I can probably stay at my mom's townhouse for a while until I find a place."

"And risk running into your dad?" He snorted. "What do you think I am? Some kind of monster to put you through that?"

"Then what do you want me to do? Because, if things are going to continue this way, then I don't think I can deal." Milo ran his fingers through his sleep-mussed hair. "Look, the last thing I want is to lose you as my friend."

Tommy rounded the counter and pulled Milo into his arms. The instinct to protest—considering Milo was naked under the robe—was strong. But for the sake of loyalty, he willed himself to relax instead.

"I don't want you to move out," Tommy whispered into his ear. "I love you as a friend too. And right now, that's more important." He stepped back and held Milo at arm's length. "But know that the second Kaz makes a mistake, I'm stepping in and I'm not letting go."

When Tommy finally used Kaz's name, it drove the point home for Milo. He also couldn't ignore the sincerity in those jade-green eyes. Making a joke didn't seem appropriate in that moment, so Milo pressed his lips together.

But after another second of silence, it seemed Milo didn't have to worry about making a joke to lighten the mood.

"Looks like you lost ten pounds since last I saw you." Tommy returned to the counter. "Good thing I brought home provisions or that guy would have fucked you to death. Who's sweet now?"

Rolling his eyes again, Milo plopped down on one of the stools and eagerly reached for the sweet and sour pork.

A part of him felt bad that Tommy was suffering from unrequited love, but another part of him—the more selfish part—was secretly happy that their friendship remained intact. Moving out was definitely an option, as much as he hated to do it, but thank God Tommy stopped him. He had nowhere else to go.

Halfway through their meal, a knock at the door interrupted their conversation. Tommy pushed off the stool and padded his way down the hall. Milo couldn't care less who was at the door in that moment. He was too busy stuffing his mouth with chow mein.

A minute later, Tommy returned with a crystal vase full of calla lilies. Milo recognized the flowers immediately. His cheeks warmed.

"Looks like someone did well last night," Tommy teased, sliding the vase onto the counter.

"Shut up!" Yet it took all of Milo's control not to hunt for the card that he knew surely came with the flowers.

Tommy beat him to it and plucked the small white envelope from a holder tucked into the bouquet. Milo jumped off the stool and snatched the note before his friend could so much as lift the flap. He turned around and slid the card out.

The warmth in his cheeks intensified to a burn that he felt all over his body.

"Come on," Tommy said. "What does it say?"

On the card with a simple gold border scrolled the words: *To be continued.*

The thoughts that assailed Milo then almost brought him to his knees. His heart leaped. He would count down the seconds with every beat until he could see Kaz again and be in his arms once more.

EVA MUÑOZ loves dreaming of worlds filled with hot guys falling in love with each other. She believes that love is love is love and everyone has a right to find their person. Her love for writing began in high school. It was because her teacher complimented a story she had written that put her on the path she is on today. She would spin yarns on her father's electric typewriter, bind the pages together, and bring the finished product to school for her classmate to pass around and swoon over. Little did she know at the time that writing would be a career she never knew she wanted.

She may have taken a circuitous path toward her passion for writing, but when she finally made that decision to stick with it after countless rejections, she never looked back. A degree in creative writing helps too. When she's not at her favorite coffee shop thinking up new worlds and characters to explore, you can find Eva in a classroom teaching creative writing of all things. Talk about passion meets day job. Today she is molding impressionable minds the way her teacher once did for her.

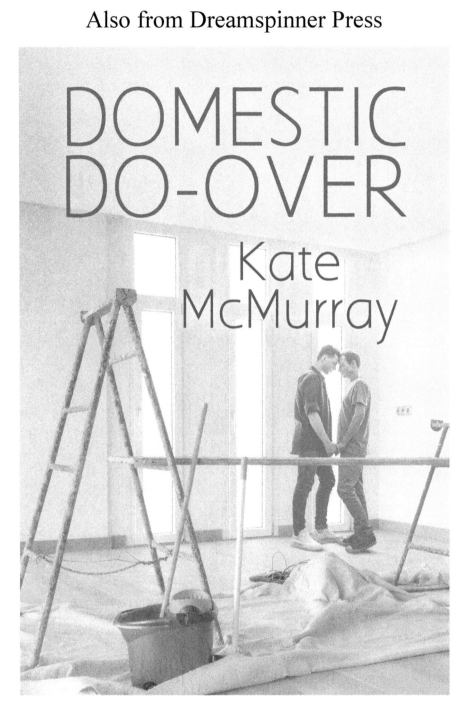

Also from Dreamspinner Press

sam carlson

A Glass of Red

"Carlson's intoxicating debut...
goes down as smoothly as a glass of
Montepulciano." —*Publishers Weekly*

www.dreamspinnerpress.com

CPSIA information can be obtained
at www.ICGtesting.com
Printed in the USA
LVHW081534301021
701978LV00019B/1054

9 781644 059302